BENT ON JUSTICE

MICHAEL ELIA

First published 2023
by Rowanvale Books Ltd
The Gate
Keppoch Street
Roath
Cardiff
CF24 3JW
www.rowanvalebooks.com

A CIP catalogue record for this book is available from the British Library.
ISBN: 978-1-914422-28-7

The Florida heat was intense over the forest overlooking a beach a few miles south of Miami. FBI Agent Dave Bradley, who along with his homicide squad in Timlook, Pennsylvania, had smashed a network of drug cartels called the New England Net in 2009, had been sent by his wife and boss, Lieutenant Nicole Lamenski, to cooperate with the FBI in Florida to nail an arms trafficking ring. It was March 2020, a few months before he would turn fifty-one; his blond hair had shades of gray creeping in, and a medium-length beard lined his still-boyish face. He was on stakeout with four long-haired vice cops, three of them bearded and one clean-shaven. The clean-shaven blond man was named Matt Cantrell. Of the bearded guys, all of whom had brown hair, Squad Leader Miles Erikson had the longest hair and sharp eyes, Matt Brogan had medium-length hair and wore glasses, and Andy Harmon had a shy smile and modest-looking eyes and features, his hair not as long as Erikson's.

Waiting in the undergrowth facing the beach, they saw an FBI plane flying from over the Gulf of Mexico to the Atlantic Ocean as it returned from Cuba.

"Let's get this right," Dave began. "That FBI plane is carrying Feds and vice cops over from Havana, who are guarding arms dealers they captured outside Guantanamo Bay?"

"A good guess," Erikson replied.

"And you reckon right." Brogan chuckled.

"We've been hunting these arms traffickers for years," Cantrell said.

"And now, we have them," Harmon growled.

"I ain't had so much fun in years." Erikson laughed.

"No," Dave said. "The fun begins when we drag them through the courts and find new leads on the arms dealers, drugs dealers and pimps who'll replace those we put away. Just wait until the airplane lands, and I'll give these guys the third degree."

The aircraft advanced through the orange-red sky. On the plane were three FBI agents, three vice cops, two pilots and the gang of handcuffed arms dealers. The pilots were a blond man and a bearded Puerto Rican. The

Feds, all in suits, were two blonde women and a mustached black guy, Sergeant Marty Hall. The vice cops were casually dressed: a dark-haired woman with sharp eyes, a blonde woman, and Squad Leader Rufus Quinn, a bearded man with long black hair. The handcuffed gun-runners were a muscular, dark-haired Cuban of forty-four named Sanchez and three Americans: a white-haired man of sixty-three; a long-haired, bearded man aged forty-one and a blonde woman who was thirty-seven.

"You see the beach ahead of us?" Hall called out.

"I see it," Quinn replied.

"We'll land on the beach and rendezvous with Erikson's guys," Hall said.

As Dave and Erikson's vice squad watched the airplane about to touch down, they heard a whooshing sound from an Army rocket launcher. A trail of smoke shot upwards, and the rocket slammed with savage violence into the plane's windshield. An ear-bursting blast exploded with deafening fury, ripping the plane apart and igniting the fuel tank. Two more blasts pulverized the plane and sent fragments of metal and glass showering over the tropical, green-blue water.

"Oh shit! What's happened?" Erikson screamed.

"I don't know!" Cantrell shouted.

"The rocket came from over there, to the right!" Harmon cried.

"And eight men are coming along the beach toward us!" Brogan growled.

"One of them with the rocket launcher which downed that plane!"

"He's loading another rocket into the bazooka," Dave said. "Open fire, now!"

Of the eight arms dealers who had destroyed the FBI plane, five had short hair, one being a sharp-eyed, dark-haired man by the name of Dextor Boyd. He and three of the others were clean-shaven whilst the fifth was bearded. The other three men were long-haired with beards, and they all wore sunglasses. Boyd, the mob leader, carried the rocket launcher whilst the others brandished high-caliber rifles.

Raising their own rifles, Dave and Erikson's squad exchanged a savage crossfire with the dealers, the cops ducking behind the trees to avoid the hail of bullets speeding toward them. Dave emerged again and repeatedly fired toward Boyd and two other mobsters, felling them with thirteen shots.

Nine gunshots from Erikson blazed toward the other two short-haired men, killing them. Cantrell, Harmon and Brogan vomited blasts from their weaponry, bringing down the three long-haired bearded guys.

"Are these guys dead?" Erikson said.

"They look very dead to me," Dave commented.

"Now we've lost Sanchez's gang," Cantrell said.

"Not to mention two pilots, three Feds and three vice cops," Erikson said. "We have the unpleasant task of breaking this news to the FBI's Florida branch, the Miami vice squad and the cops' families."

"Leave that job to that evil cut-throat, Chief Gary Mills," Dave advised. "And the more conscientious black man below him with more sound ethics, Captain Robert Siffrey."

"You've latched on to what a barracuda Gary Mills is?" Erikson asked.

"Let's put it this way. With a piece of work like Mills running Homicide in Florida, how evil do the arms dealers have to be? Including Dextor Boyd, who fired the bazooka which downed that plane to kill Sanchez and his three dealers. Not to mention the two pilots, three Feds and three vice cops under Hall and Quinn who had the lousy luck to be on that plane. Now we must call Forensics and CSI, collect the weapons from Boyd's mob, detail the serial numbers and trace them to another dealer."

They hurried out from between the trees and approached the dead arms dealers.

***

FBI Agent Tony Selma was a young man of twenty-seven with short blond hair, a mustache and glasses. He was dressed in jeans, a blue T-shirt and a brown leather jacket. He was with five vice cops, staking out a liquor store in the respectable Miami suburb of Biscayne, overlooking Biscayne Bay, which leads out into the Atlantic. The vice cops were two well-built black men with mustaches; a long-haired Puerto Rican with Asian features and a medium-length mustache; an overweight black woman with long, wavy hair, and a young, skinny black man with a thin mustache, all casually dressed like Tony.

One of the well-built black men in their late forties was Squad Leader Barry Ritchie, whilst the young man smiling was named Nathan Dill. Tony and Dill were positioned inside the office at the back of the store while the others were situated near the till. There had been armed raids on liquor stores throughout Florida, and the state's national phone line had intercepted a call saying this store in Biscayne was the gang's next target. Tony Selma and Barry Ritchie hadn't hesitated to drive there immediately, hide the squad van in a side street and then stake out the store.

"This stakeout had better be worth it," Tony said.

"We may have a long wait, man," Dill replied.

"Or maybe not. I hear a van outside the front of the store."

"The van's arrived, and it's heavily armored, like a smash-and-grab vehicle about to do a bank job," Ritchie said from the till.

"Looks mighty suspicious," Dill whispered.

"It's now or never," Tony said.

Inside the armored van, three men were sat in the front seats. One was a mustached black man and two were long-haired white men, one dark-haired and the other blond.

Positioned in the back seats were a forty-two-year-old guy with long gray hair wearing a cowboy hat, a bearded man with short dark hair and sinister eyes, and four bearded Cubans.

"Ready to make the hit?" the black man asked.

"I'm ready," the driver said. "Let's make our move."

Banging his keys into the ignition, he reversed the van across the street, then charged at full speed toward the liquor store and smashed the armored vehicle through the window. Brandishing their high-velocity rifles, the nine men scrambled out of the vehicle and fired at the four undercover cops at the till, who ducked. Seizing their rifles, the cops blasted the raiders with several gunshots, killing the cowboy and the four Cubans. Five blasts from the black woman brought down the bearded guy with black hair, but the three ringleaders returned ferocious rifle fire with extreme violence, shooting and shooting, until the woman, the Puerto Rican and the black man dropped to the floor, riddled with bullets. Ritchie tried to retaliate again, but the blond mob leader pumped two shots into his chest, smearing his jacket with blood and sending him falling onto the other three vice cops.

The three mobsters left alive bashed open the till, but Tony and Dill hurried out of the office, focused their high-powered rifles and blazed savage gunfire. Dill sent three slugs into the black mobster while Tony pumped two rounds into the dark-haired gangster. Both raiders fell to the ground and died in hideous rivers of blood. The blond ringleader spun toward both young men with his rifle raised, but Tony fired three bullets into the guy's chest and abdomen, and he crumpled to the floor, blood soaking his shirt and jacket.

"Ritchie!" Dill exclaimed. "Oh shit, man! They're all dead!"

"Damn it!" Tony cursed. "I'll call Forensics."

***

At Miami Police Department, Chief Gary Mills and Captain Robert Siffrey stood inside Siffrey's office, flanked by Lieutenants Ken Ross and Alex Smith. All four men were middle-aged, tall and bearded, Mills and Smith having short gray hair and Ross long dark hair. Siffrey was a slim black man.

Chief Mills spotted Dave Bradley, Erikson's vice squad, Dill, and Tony Selma entering the main office and turned to Captain Siffrey. "Tell the two Feds and the men from Vice I want them in your office now!" he demanded, his tone aggressive.

"Don't be too hard on them, Chief," Captain Siffrey pleaded, rubbing his beard.

Mills, Ross and Smith bristled with rage.

"Are you giving me orders?" Mills yelled.

"No, it's a request," Captain Siffrey told him.

"We lost Sanchez's gang of four!" Ross screamed.

"And three teams of Feds and vice cops!" Smith shouted.

"We have no time to pussyfoot around!"

"So, get these men in here now!" Mills bellowed.

Siffrey, intimidated, pulled open his office door.

"Agents Dave Bradley and Tony Selma," Siffrey said. "We want you in my office. Vice cops Erikson, Cantrell, Brogan, Harmon and Dill, you come over too. I sure wouldn't want to be in your shoes, man."

"You can dispense with the pleasantries, Captain," Mills snapped, his tone condescending.

"This doesn't look good," Dave commented on his way into the office.

"It sure doesn't," Tony replied.

"Are you giving us another grilling, Chief?" Erikson wanted to know. "Because we did everything by the book. Nobody could've predicted Dextor Boyd's gang would be lying in wait for the FBI plane."

"Who cares if we lost Sanchez's gang?" Brogan asked.

"Spare a thought for Marty Hall, Rufus Quinn and their teams who were on that plane," Harmon said.

"We're deeply upset." Brogan steadied his glasses.

"Although Sanchez's mob died, we can find other means of smashing Florida's arms rings," Cantrell protested.

"And our termination of Dextor Boyd's men was self-defense," Harmon said.

"And by the book," Brogan added.

"Boyd was about to use the same rocket launcher against us that he used to down that plane," Erikson said.

"I fired the shots that killed Dextor Boyd and two of his men," Dave told Mills.

"Have you all quite finished?" Mills snapped.

"Yes, sir."

"And you, Federal Agent Tony Selma and vice cop Nathan Dill," Mills began again.

"What about us?" Tony asked.

"You wiped out a whole mob of store raiders?" Mills asked, his manner aggressive. "Is this true?"

"It is, sir."

"You were meant to take them alive! Instead, your vice squad got into a shootout, and four vice cops, including Squad Leader Barry Ritchie, are dead! Only you and this punk of a kid survived!"

"Hey, don't call me a punk!" Dill objected.

"It's okay," Tony promised him. "I'll take responsibility."

"Dill is a kid who has much to learn!" Mills said. "But you, Agent Selma! How old are you?"

"I'm twenty-seven."

"And your years?" Mills asked. "Stop right there! You, Matt Cantrell, are in your late thirties! Vice cops Brogan and Harmon are in their mid-to-late forties! Squad Leader Miles Erikson is in his early fifties! How old are you, Agent Bradley?"

"Fifty," Dave informed him.

"You all acted like youthful amateurs!" Mills yelled. "If you two Feds from Pennsylvania want to uphold the law here in Florida, you don't operate a private army of cowboy cops like John Wayne! If that ever causes a problem for you, go back to Timlook and run amok in your own jurisdiction! You got that?"

"We got it," Dave and Tony responded.

"I have some business to attend to at my place at Little Havana with Lieutenants Ross and Smith," Mills said.

"Some business?" Brogan enquired.

"What kind of business?" Harmon asked.

"Business which lines our pockets with big money," Mills retorted. "Really big money."

"More like dirty money confiscated from arms dealers," Cantrell commented.

"That's enough, Cantrell!" Erikson growled.

"Sorry, sir."

"We're leaving, guys," Mills told Ross and Smith.

The bearded brutes vacated the captain's office and headed through the main office toward the entrance.

"Don't take it personally," Captain Siffrey reassured Dave and Tony. "Those three have the conduct and moral consciences of barracudas."

Then five other vice cops—two men and three women—came to Siffrey's office door.

"Agents Bradley and Selma," Siffrey said. "You haven't met the rest of Erikson's vice squad. Five outstanding cops who are decorated for bravery. Nine men and women altogether in Erikson's team. One more will join them: Nathan Dill."

"Thank you, Captain." A smile reached both sides of Dill's mustached face.

"These five cops are Eddie Gierek, John Orion, Amy Cantrell, Helen Post and Patricia Hayes," Siffrey continued. "You guys, follow me outside my office, and Bradley and Selma will introduce themselves."

Selma followed behind Erikson's vice squad, but Dave stood rooted to the floor.

These men and women were casually dressed in jeans and untidy shirts. Eddie Gierek was well-muscled and clean-shaven with long gray hair, whilst John Orion was muscular with long, reddish-brown hair and a thick beard. Both men were in their late thirties.

But Dave was struck by the insane beauty of the three young women. Aged twenty-eight, Amy Cantrell was the spitting image of the DEA agent played by Emily Blunt in the 2015 drugs war thriller *Sicario*. She had dark hair tied back in a ponytail, exposing her forehead, and she wore neutral lipstick that did not stand out. Also attractive, but no great beauty, Helen Post had long brown hair, a feminine face and a bright grin, but no makeup. She was thirty-two years old. And Patricia Hayes, aged twenty-seven, was as pretty as Amy. She closely resembled the actress Demi Moore in her younger years when she'd starred in *Indecent Proposal* in 1992 and *Disclosure* in 1996. Her shiny black hair was in a ponytail, her intelligent eyes made her look professional, and dark lipstick covered her lips.

"Come on, Dave," Tony insisted.

"I'm coming," Dave said.

They introduced themselves to the two men and three women.

"We've come over from Timlook, Pennsylvania to assist your vice squad in nailing arms rings here in Florida," Tony explained. "Due to Barry Ritchie's vice squad being massacred in that liquor store shootout, the only survivor, Nathan Dill, will join your vice squad."

"It will be a pleasure to have him," the bearded cop said. "I'm Officer John Orion."

"Officer Eddie Gierek," said the gray-haired man.

"I'm Officer Amy Cantrell, Matt Cantrell's wife," the brunette told Dave and Tony.

"I'm Officer Helen Post," the brown-haired lady said.

"And Officer Patricia Hayes," the pretty black-haired woman finished off.

"Can we refer to you by your first names?" Helen asked. "Or do you prefer Agents Bradley and Selma?"

"We prefer Dave and Tony," Dave replied.

"You heard about the two massacres?" Tony enquired.

"We did," Orion said. "Our sympathy does nothing to alleviate this tragedy, especially for Officer Dill who witnessed Squad Leader Ritchie's people being shot to death."

"But we're sorry, all the same," Gierek told the young black man.

"Sympathy is the last thing I want," Dill said. "I just want to get on with the job."

"That's the best way to look at it," Gierek remarked. "But we collected two lots of info from the DNA profiles of the dead arms dealers and store raiders at both crime scenes, not to mention the rocket launcher and the rifles confiscated by Forensics. By the serial numbers on the weapons, we traced them to two Cuban arms dealers in North Beach and Biscayne. Luis Calvera and Ramon Batista, both close associates in the underworld of arms and drugs dealing. Both men are violent and extremely dangerous and won't scruple to shoot at cops. Dextor Boyd's gang was working for Calvera and bought their weapons from him. The store raiders in the armored van at Biscayne were paid by and bought their rifles and ammo from Batista. We have printed information on these links, and also the DNA profiles of both gangs downloaded from our database. All the connections of one mob lead to Calvera and all the connections of the other lead to Batista.

"To maintain our cover in the Underworld, none of us vice cops can approach Calvera and Batista."

"Your job, Dave, Tony," Captain Siffrey finished, "is to throw the book at Calvera and Batista."

"We're on our way," Dave said.

***

At a lavish estate across the highway from North Beach, Dave and Tony left their civilian car, covered the distance down the driveway, and Dave knocked his fist hard against Luis Calvera's front door. After five seconds, a stocky Cuban with a thick mustache opened the door and frowned menacingly at the Feds.

"What do you want?" the brute growled.

"We're FBI," Dave announced. "I'm Agent Dave Bradley."

"And I'm Agent Tony Selma."

"Is Luis Calvera in?" Dave asked.

"You're talking to him," the mustached Cuban said. "And I'm busy looking at my bank statements."

"This will only take a few minutes," Dave told him. "Can we come in? Or we'll have to arrest you and drag you down to the police department."

"Come in," Calvera agreed. "Make it five minutes."

The Feds followed Calvera through the hallway into a posh dining room. He was alone.

"I noticed something," Dave said. "There are no armed men or bodyguards protecting your premises. And you're alone in this building."

"I'm not the Mafia or a drug lord who breaks the law," Calvera said. "All my activities are legal. And as a Cuban arms dealer who protects the peace between Cuba and the United States, I have diplomatic immunity, until I do something illegal. And none of you cops will ever prove my involvement in any murder or any form of skullduggery, so I'm an untouchable. Another thing. The peace between Cuba and the United States is a fragile peace, and due to my diplomatic immunity, if you harass me or my people or arrest us, you could bring both countries close to war. Drug dealing is illegal. So is murder. But arms dealing is legal. Cuban arms dealers like me pass weapons between Cuba and America to fight terrorists and drug lords in South America.

"If you persecute and arrest me or my people, the vital sale of weapons between both countries will cease. With the backing of Mexico, countries in South America and the Middle East, and also Russia and China, Cuba could start a war with America. Or it could supply arms to terrorist organizations and drug cartels to commit evil crimes against American citizens, in America and throughout the world. That's why your government and my government protect me.

"Drug lords compete with each other and kill each other. Arms dealers don't. Because no Mafia or drug dealers or arms dealers have a reason to threaten me, I don't need bodyguards to protect me. That's the reason nobody challenged you when you walked down my drive. And I'm alone because I like my own company and don't mix well in groups, except with my fellow dealers."

"You've made yourself clear," Dave told Calvera. "But I have a few questions."

"Make it fast."

"This morning," Dave said, "an FBI plane carrying three Feds, three vice cops and four arms dealers was about to rendezvous with a team of police officers including myself on a beach south of Miami when it was shot down with an Army rocket launcher by American arms dealers led by Dextor Boyd. All ten passengers died. My men then killed Boyd and his mob in a shootout on the beach."

"I've never heard of Dextor Boyd," Calvera growled. "And you told me they were Americans, not Cubans. American arms dealers have a reason to kill innocent people or cops if they break America's laws and want to cover up their crimes. Which is ironic, because when America's gun lobbies and gun stores sell guns to American citizens, the Constitution defends the right to bear arms. It's none of my business if American arms dealers kill American or foreign citizens."

"Then how do you explain the fact you sold the Army rocket launcher and the rifles to Boyd's mob?" Dave asked. "The weapons used to down the FBI plane and then to fire at my team of officers on the beach. You have heard of Dextor Boyd. When we took down the weapons' serial numbers, we traced the weapons back to you and your mobsters. We also ran DNA samples from the eight dead arms dealers through our DNA database, and all of Dextor Boyd's mob had close links with your mob. And the four arms dealers, including Sanchez, who were on that FBI plane being extradited from Cuba to Florida were also connected to your mob and would testify against your illegal arms dealing in Cuba and Florida. That's the reason you sent Dextor Boyd's men to massacre them.

"Dextor Boyd and his mob are no longer around to testify against you, but if I were you, I'd play your diplomatic immunity card correctly. It won't protect you forever. Especially if we find out you sold weapons illegally and killed more people in America and Cuba, so the Cuban government loses its incentive to protect you."

"Another thing," Tony said. "When you invited us onto your premises, you told us you were looking at your bank statements. A millionaire arms dealer like you shouldn't be having money problems. Especially when I can see on these statements your offshore account is in the Bahamas, where nobody can touch your money. If anybody has tried to steal your money, we can arrest them for extortion or a lesser crime and get this person or people out of your way. If you do us a favor."

"A favor, señor," Calvera sneered.

"You mention nothing to the Cuban government or the Cuban Embassy about our investigations into crimes committed by American or Cuban arms dealers in Florida," Tony ordered. "It's not worth destroying the fragile peace between Cuba and the United States."

"I'll tell you why I was looking at my bank statements, and Ramon Batista's bank statements, too," Calvera explained.

"Miami PD has known for years you have close links with Ramon Batista," Dave said. "But carry on."

"You're scared of your millions of dollars disappearing," Tony told Calvera. "Which is why you keep checking your bank statements. I know somebody's after your money. Another arms dealer or organized criminal."

"A cop is after my money in the Bahamas," Calvera said. "By the name of Chief Gary Mills. He is in his late fifties, tall and strongly built with short gray hair and a beard. He has a temper like a cornered alligator. Two days ago, he paid me a visit and threatened me with a .45 Magnum, the handgun Clint Eastwood used in his *Dirty Harry* movies. You argue with a cop, but not with a .45 Magnum. He demanded to know my PIN number and the bank details of my offshore account in the Bahamas. I wrote down this information, which he then stole and exited my premises. I was shaken up really badly. When I phoned my bank at Nassau in the Bahamas and reported the incident, they refused to believe me and would not change my PIN number or bank details. So, every time I look at my bank statements, I cower at the thought that

Chief Mills or people working for him have dug their dirty hands into my millions."

"We'll pass this information onto the Feds," Dave promised the mustached mobster. "Thank you for your time, Luis. We'd better shoot off."

Dave and Tony rose from the settee and vacated the estate. They made their way toward their civilian FBI car. Dave deactivated the locking system, and both Feds opened the front doors and climbed inside, Dave pressing his keys into the ignition.

"What do we tell the Feds about Chief Mills' visit to Calvera?" Tony asked. "Mills is ruthless and brutal, but is he really corrupt?"

"He combines all three vices in a matchless ratio," Dave remarked. "So even if you think Calvera's allegation against Mills is false, I know it's the truth. Otherwise, Calvera wouldn't be terrified of his Bahamas account disappearing."

"Do we tell the Feds?" Tony wanted to know. "And if so, when?"

"We don't tell the Feds anything," Dave said. "We're not after Chief Mills. We're after Calvera and Batista. When we've smashed the arms rings behind those two massacres and nailed these two mobsters, we wait until

Mills does something really criminal. And then tell the Feds."

"Our next stop, Biscayne," Tony told Dave. "Where we weasel the truth out of Ramon Batista. The liquor store massacre was my team, so let me do the interrogation."

"I get that," Dave said.

***

In Biscayne, they left the civilian car, made their way down the driveway to Batista's estate, and Dave thumped the front door.

"You notice the same thing here as at Calvera's estate?" Tony asked Dave.

"No armed men or bodyguards challenging us," Dave said. "Calvera told us a pack of lies, but he was right about one thing. Because arms dealing is legal, Cuban arms dealers have diplomatic immunity and don't compete or fight over territory or money; they don't waste money on hiring armed guards. The armed men in their arms rings are enough to protect them. But I don't hear or see people through the door or windows talking or shouting. Meaning Batista is alone. And he's coming. Are you ready?"

A tall Cuban with long hair and a thick beard pulled open the front door and stared at the Feds with brutal hostility in his eyes.

"Who are you?" he snapped.

"FBI Agents Dave Bradley and Tony Selma," Dave replied. "Are you Ramon Batista?"

"Si, señor." Batista's glaring eyes became fiery with rage. "I have nothing to say to you."

"Then we'll thrust the handcuffs on and run you down to Miami PD," Dave threatened. "But if you answer our questions, this will only take a few minutes."

"I'm ready to give you the third degree," Tony growled.

"Come in," Batista said.

They entered his premises and followed him into the dining room.

"I'll ask the questions," Tony reminded Dave.

"Go on," Dave told him.

"We see bank statements on your table," Tony addressed Batista. "Sent to you from your offshore bank in Nassau in the Bahamas."

The expression on Batista's brutish face was one of sheer shock.

"How do you know I have an offshore account in the Bahamas?"

"Your associate in the underworld, Luis Calvera, has an offshore account on these islands," Tony explained. "We dropped in on Calvera and interrogated him a few minutes ago. Calvera was sweating with terror that his millions of dollars would start disappearing, so he was obsessively checking his bank statements. There are only three places on this earth where nobody, not even the law, can touch your money in offshore accounts. Geneva in Switzerland, the Grand Cayman Islands and the Bahamas. Not unless somebody discovers your PIN number and bank details, pretends to represent you and wires your money from your account over to theirs. Which is illegal. But according to Calvera, two days ago, a cop with gray hair and a beard entered his premises and threatened him with a .45 Magnum. And extorted info from Calvera about his PIN number and bank details. He took a sheet of paper with this info from Calvera and left the premises. Calvera then phoned his bank to report this, but they refused to believe him or to change his PIN number and bank details.

"Calvera had also been checking some of your bank statements to see if any of your money had gone missing. Did Calvera's terrifying experience with this dirty cop also happen to you, Ramon? Don't lie to me. Nobody can touch your money in the Bahamas, so why are there bank statements covering your dinner table. Like you're scared."

"I'll tell you," Batista hissed.

"Did a cop threaten you?" Tony asked.

"With a .45 Magnum?" Dave said.

"Si, señor, yes."

"Can you describe him?"

"He was in his late fifties, tall and muscled with short gray hair and a beard," Batista told them. "At first, he knocked on my door and appeared friendly. Then he pulled out the .45 Magnum and threatened to pop me with a double tap to the head if I didn't tell him my PIN number and bank details. I wrote down the info for him and he left the premises."

"Did he give his name?" Tony asked.

"Chief Gary Mills," Batista replied.

"When did this happen and at what time?" Tony demanded.

"Two days ago, at 11 a.m. Half an hour after he intimidated Calvera and extorted from my associate his PIN Number and bank details, he stole mine."

"How do you know Calvera's ordeal was half an hour before yours?" Tony snapped. "Calvera must've phoned or bleeped you."

"I phoned Calvera after Chief Mills attacked and threatened me," Batista said. "And Calvera told me Gary Mills had threatened him at 10:30 a.m., half an hour before he drove over here and threatened me. What will you do about this guy Mills?"

"We may consider reporting him to the FBI and let the Feds deal with him," Tony said. "Or we may not. We'll consider it on two conditions, the same conditions we imposed on Calvera. We know Cuban arms dealers like you and Calvera have diplomatic immunity here in Florida. This means in order not to upset the fragile peace and the legal arms trade between Cuba and America, American law enforcement cannot harass or arrest Cuban arms dealers. To do this would either start a war between both countries or end the legal arms trade, so the Cubans could get back at the Americans by selling arms to international terrorist organizations or to drug cartels in Cuba, Mexico and South America. Weapons which would be used to attack American civilians or American troops in this country or abroad. But this diplomatic immunity you have only applies if your arms rings are not behind attacks on American law enforcement or selling arms to terrorist organizations or other criminal organizations in the United States. That's condition number one. Condition number two is you tell us the truth about a gang of nine store raiders who attacked a liquor store here in Biscayne, a mile from here. And don't lie to me, Ramon. Calvera sent eight arms dealers including the mob leader Dextor Boyd to shoot down an FBI plane with a bazooka, to silence four arms dealers including the Cuban mob leader Sanchez. These mobsters, together with the two pilots, three Feds and three vice cops, perished in that attack. Calvera tried to lie to us, saying he never sent Boyd to down that plane, but the mob's DNA profiles and the weapons' serial numbers linked these eight men to Calvera.

"About the nine men who attacked that liquor store. After Florida's national phone line intercepted an incriminating cell phone call between two of the men, me and five cops lay in wait in this store, and when the mob attacked, we killed them. Four cops died, but two of us are still alive. On collecting the store raiders' DNA and recording the weapons' serial numbers, we discovered these men were working for your mob and using rifles you sold to them. Give me one good reason why we shouldn't run you into the joint right now."

"Okay, okay!" Batista cried.

"I'm listening, Ramon."

"I did sell those weapons! And those store raiders were linked to my arms ring! But we had no knowledge these men would attack that liquor store! Neither me nor my people sent these men to execute this brutal violence! Hundreds of foreign arms dealers in America break the law, finance terrorists and organized criminals, and kill people. Maybe Calvera has done this. But my actions are within the law."

"I believe you. Millions wouldn't," Tony growled. "From now on, you and your people better keep your noses clean. Or your diplomatic immunity will run out. Especially if the Cuban government finds out you murdered people in Cuba as well as in America. We'll run a check on Chief Mills and twist Mills' arm to leave you, Calvera and your bank accounts alone. Or get the Feds to deal with him."

"Okay, Tony," Dave said. "Let's head back to base."

***

At Chief Gary Mills' place in Little Havana, Mills was pulling a deal with Lieutenants Ken Ross and Alex Smith.

"Okay, Gary," Ross began. "You talked about big money."

"At Miami PD," Smith added.

"Two days ago," Chief Mills said, "I visited the estates of Luis Calvera and Ramon Batista. I threatened them with a .45 Magnum and forced them to give me their PIN numbers and bank details. Both mobsters have offshore bank accounts in the Bahamas, at a bank in Nassau. Both accounts contain a total of three hundred million dollars, most of it drugs money and arms money. Each of us will have a hundred million dollars of this money. I want both of you to take the next airline flight to the Bahamas, then take a speedboat to Nassau and wire this money by direct bank transfer to my bank account in Orlando. Tell the bank workers that Luis Calvera and Ramon Batista are working for me and sent you to transfer this money on their behalf. These papers with the bank details I stole from them are forged to look like they willingly forfeited this information. Take them with you. When the job is done, you take the next flight back to Miami. And that three hundred million dollars is ours."

All three men laughed.

***

Once their airliner had touched down in the Bahamas, Ross and Smith were driven to a remote location on a beach famous for speedboats. They paid for a speedboat, then raced the vessel across the water to another island and circled the island until they reached Nassau. Leaving the boat, they headed into this modern city and found the bank. They approached the bank manager, who was a middle-aged, overweight black woman.

"Can I help you?" she asked.

"We're working for Gary Mills, Luis Calvera and Ramon Batista," Ross said.

"Calvera and Batista sent us to wire their money over to a law firm they're working for in Orlando, Florida," Smith continued. "Gary Mills runs this law firm."

"I've never heard of no law firm in Orlando, Florida," the manager said. "Do you have concrete evidence to prove Calvera and Batista sent you to wire this money?"

"Here's written information," Ross told her. "Papers with their PIN numbers and bank details passed onto us. There are three signatures on both papers from Mills, Calvera and Batista. On these papers, Calvera has a hundred and seventy million dollars and Batista a hundred and thirty million. Three hundred million bucks in total."

Both lieutenants knew how Chief Mills had read the mobsters' handwriting on both papers and faked their signatures to provide phony evidence they had given consent.

"You see, two of these three signatures are consistent with the Cubans' handwriting and the third signature is from Mills," Ross pointed out. "Can you transfer this money to Florida?"

"We'll transfer it straight away," the woman said.

***

Three hours later, Ross and Smith boarded the flight for Miami.

They lowered themselves into the fifth row of seats on the plane's left side. Ross heard his cell phone bleeping.

"You'd better answer that," Smith suggested.

Ross raised the phone to his bearded face. "Hi there. Is that Chief Mills?"

"It's your chief," Mills replied. "How did it go?"

"It was a piece of cake." Ross chuckled.

"The bank manager in Nassau fell for the con." Smith laughed.

"The money was wired through to your bank account in Orlando," Ross told him. "We must take a trip to Orlando and split the three hundred million three ways between us. We're on the plane and we'll arrive in Miami in less than one or two hours."

"When you arrive," Mills said, "I have some unfinished business concerning FBI Agents Bradley and Selma. Bradley and Selma are dangerous. They always smash criminal cases wide open, and sooner or later they'll hatch onto our greed and corruption. Matt Cantrell hatched on before they did. When I was abusive in the captain's office toward these two Feds and Miles Erikson's guys, I let it slip out that the three of us were cutting a deal at my place involving big money, really big money. Cantrell made a remark about dirty money confiscated from arms dealers."

"It was an off-the-cuff remark, Chief," Ross added. "Cantrell and Erikson's guys know nothing about this."

"Maybe. They're tough, but stupid," Mills pointed out. "But Agents Bradley and Selma are not stupid. A kid detective like Selma has brains, but a middle-aged guy like Bradley has brains and experience. Even if Erikson's guys including Cantrell fail to smell corruption, Bradley and Selma will. That black bastard Captain Robert Siffrey is also dangerous, although not as dangerous as Bradley and Selma. Captain Siffrey is dangerous because he's honest and cannot be corrupted."

"What must we do?" Ross asked.

"Lie low," Mills replied. "For now, we keep a low profile until Bradley and Selma lower their guard."

"Have it your way, Chief."

"The air hostess is coming," Smith told Ross. "Better switch off your cell. Calls aren't allowed on air flights."

"I'd better break off the call," Ross told Mills. "Good day." He hung up.

***

At Miami PD, Dave and Tony informed Squad Leader Erikson's team about Chief Mills's potentially violent assault on Calvera and Batista, and how it was only a matter of time before Mills, with the aid of their bank details, would wire their money through to his bank account.

"The son of a bitch!" Patricia screamed.

"Mills played us all along!" Amy snapped.

"I took Mills to be an arrogant and abusive bully, but never a dirty cop," Helen said.

"With scum like Mills running our outfit…" Patricia started.

"…How evil do the criminals have to be?" Amy finished for her.

"That's my line," Dave objected.

"What you said on the beach after we killed Dextor Boyd's mob," Brogan told him.

"So, Cantrell was right," Harmon remarked.

"Right about what?" Gierek asked.

Erikson answered. "When Mills bullied us in the captain's office, Mills then told us he, Ross and Smith had to pull a deal at his place regarding really big money."

"Where does Officer Cantrell come in?" Helen asked.

"I remarked about dirty money confiscated from arms dealers," Cantrell replied.

"And you were right, Matt," Amy praised him.

"How did you figure this out?" Patricia enquired.

"Was it a hunch?" Tony asked.

"It wasn't a hunch," Dave said.

"How did he know?" Dill asked.

"He didn't figure it out, and it wasn't a hunch or even a guess."

"Just a careless wind-up remark in retaliation for Mills abusing you guys," Orion finished.

"You got it," Erikson growled.

"But I was right," Cantrell protested. "About dirty money stolen from arms dealers."

"Otherwise, why did Mills point a .45 Magnum in the Cubans' faces and steal their PIN numbers and bank details?" Brogan objected.

"If his target ain't their two offshore accounts in the Bahamas?" Tony butted in.

"We mustn't jump to conclusions yet," Gierek continued. "Without all the facts, supposition is a very dangerous thing and can bring deadly repercussions onto all of us. But we can't walk away from this either."

"I suggest for now, we just lie low," Dave decided.

"Just lie low?" Amy complained.

"And keep a low profile," Erikson added.

"Keep a low profile?"

"You must be kidding, right?" Helen said.

"I'm not kidding, ladies," Dave finished off. "We start throwing accusations against Chief Mills based on supposition, we'll face disciplinary action from a higher authority more powerful than Mills, and we'll be lucky not to go to jail, let alone lose our jobs."

"In the meantime…" Orion growled.

"Where is Captain Siffrey?" Gierek asked.

"Visiting hillbilly cops with beards and mustaches at a secret apartment on South Beach," Cantrell said.

"Their beards are as thick as Siffrey's beard, thicker than Bradley's beard, but not as thick as mine," Erikson replied.

"Those bearded vice cops are Officers Jeris Bridgeman, Harper Jones, Jake Chambers and Rudy Foxworth!" Patricia shouted.

"Hey, hey!" Erikson exclaimed. "You don't have to shout my head off, Hayes!"

"What are Captain Siffrey and these vice cops doing at that secret apartment?" Dave asked.

"Protecting two Cuban women who are informants ratting on Calvera's people," Harmon said.

"But their names are confidential," Brogan told Dave.

"Classified information," Dave agreed. "Officers Orion, Gierek, Amy Cantrell, Post and Hayes, I suggest we drop in on Lieutenants Ken Ross and Alex Smith, and bring Chief Mills's corruption to their attention and hear their advice before going to the Feds. But we'll have our lunches first and a flask of coffee. Is that okay by you, Squad Leader?"

"It's okay by me," Erikson replied.

***

At Little Havana, Chief Mills telephoned Captain Siffrey's cell, and Siffrey answered. Siffrey was at the secret apartment with the two Cuban women and four vice cops, Jeris Bridgeman, Harper Jones, Jake Chambers and Rudy Foxworth. Bridgeman was fair-haired and Jones was blond whilst Chambers was brown-haired and Foxworth had black hair. The informants they were protecting were small in height, one slim and the other overweight. All six men and women waited anxiously as Siffrey answered the call.

"Captain Robert Siffrey here. Can I help you?"

"It's Chief Gary Mills. Captain Siffrey, I have an enquiry."

"Go on."

"Are you at Miami PD? If not, where can I meet you? I must meet with the two women informants you're protecting so they can pass on to me the info they told you."

"We're at Dace Apartment on South Beach."

"Dace Apartment," Mills confirmed. "I'll meet you in half an hour."

He hung up, then he dialed Luis Calvera's cell and instantly received an answer.

"Luis Calvera here."

"I have some information, Luis," Mills told him.

"After you intimidated me and Batista on our premises and stole our bank details?" Calvera shouted. "That's the ultimate double-cross!"

"About your PIN numbers and bank details," Mills said. "Captain Robert Siffrey confiscated them from me. He sent FBI Agents Dave Bradley and Tony Selma to Nassau in the Bahamas, and they wired your three hundred million dollars through to Siffrey's bank account here in Miami. Captain Siffrey paid Bradley and Selma handsome sums of money for this. But I can have your money returned to you if you get Siffrey, Bradley and Selma out of the way."

"Where are they?" Calvera asked. His voice was aggressive and rude.

"Bradley and Selma will come in and out of Miami PD regularly," Mills told him. "Captain Siffrey is at the Dace Apartment overlooking South Beach, number thirty-seven."

"Dace Apartment on South Beach!" Calvera growled. "Two gangs of my men are on their way! And don't double-cross or intimidate me, Batista or my people again, Mills! Or your treachery will draw in the sharks like blood! Good day!"

He hung up.

***

Dave, Tony, Gierek and Orion were flanked by Amy, Helen and Patricia as they approached their squad van in the car park. Stalking them from behind was a mob of bearded Cubans.

One Cuban addressed the mob leader. "We should be carrying rifles and automatic weapons to waste these people, not knives," he whispered. "With knives, we must get up close to them."

"After those two massacres on the beach and in the liquor store," the mob leader said, "the cops traced the mobsters' weapons back to Calvera and Batista. But flick-knives have no serial numbers. The cops will think a street gang of youths with a violent grudge committed this mass murder. Let's get them!"

The mob charged, but the cops reacted fast, self-defense reflexes swinging into action. With his kung fu, Dave turned and swung a fast sideways kick into the mob leader's leg just above the knee. The mob leader screamed in agony as his thigh bone snapped like a tree branch. Tony threw his foot into a second man's stomach, rupturing his insides so the brute fell to the concrete clutching his midriff. Four other men went for Orion and Gierek, but kicks to the knees of two men broke their legs. Orion and Gierek seized the knife-wielding arms of the other two crooks and twisted them violently, the criminals' arms ripping out of the sockets in their shoulders.

Three thugs pounced on Dave and Tony as two more swiped their flick-knives toward Orion and Gierek. Tony's fist smashed brutally into a crook's face and split his jaw open whilst five blows from Dave's fist knocked one criminal's teeth from his gums and broke another criminal's nose. Blood gushed down the men's faces. Orion's fist caught one guy in the throat, killing him instantly, whilst Gierek's two punches split open another's nose, a torrent of blood pouring down the brute's face. With two lethal kicks, Amy gouged a man's groin and Patricia dislocated a kneecap.

The attackers yelled and hollered on the ground, their faces smeared with blood, others screaming with appalling agony as they hit the floor.

Three other mobsters went for Amy, Helen and Patricia, pulling violently on the women's hair. Amy and Patricia's ponytails came loose and their hair dropped down over their faces, their foreheads wrinkling as they screamed with pain. Helen also screamed as her hair was wrenched with force, but she maintained her balance. Amy stabbed her fingernails into a killer's eyes just as Helen thrust a deadly hand strike into a mobster's nose and Patricia punched a third brute in the throat, snapping his windpipe. In the five seconds it took for Patricia's attacker to die, Amy and Helen rained punches into the other two opponents, one mobster suffering blows to the groin and face, the other blows to the solar plexus, head and eyes. Both men collapsed.

Although badly injured, the mobsters still alive fought their agony and forced themselves to their feet, grabbing their flick-knives again to throw toward Dave, Tony, Orion and Gierek. The male cops had no time to pull out their handguns before the mobsters sent their blades flying with lightning speed.

"Get down!" Dave yelled.

The policemen dropped, the knives flying above them and bouncing off the squad van. Amy, Helen and Patricia yanked out their handguns from their leather jackets, but reinforcements of vice cops got to the mobsters first. Hearing the screaming, crying and fighting from inside the department, Officers Dill and Erikson together with Cantrell, Brogan and Harmon raced out of the building with handguns raised and blazed a hail of gunshots toward the mobsters. All but one of the brutes died in a matter of seconds, blood spattering their leather jackets.

"Don't shoot that guy!" Dave shouted. "I must interrogate him!"

"Hold your fire!" Erikson ordered the other four vice cops.

"What's Bradley doing?" Dill asked.

Dave scrambled to his feet, seized the last mobster by the lapels of his leather jacket and shouted violently. "Who sent you guys to knife us? And why?"

"Luis Calvera," the guy mumbled, blood gushing out of his mouth. "Captain Siffrey sent you and Agent Selma to the Bahamas to wire the mob's money through to his bank account. Siffrey stole Calvera's money, and Calvera wants all three of you dead."

Then the man's eyes closed forlornly and he died outright.

"Hey, hey, hey!" Dave cried. "Wake up! Wake up!"

"He's gone!" Erikson said.

"Siffrey and the four vice cops are in danger!" Tony warned Dave.

"We must head for Dace Apartment on South Beach now," Dave decided. "Tony, get in the van's front seat—I'll drive. Orion, Gierek and you three women, come with us. One of you get on to your cell phone and call Siffrey!"

Orion and Gierek along with Amy, Patricia and Helen scrambled through the squad van's side doors as Dave and Tony leaped into the front seats, Dave punching his keys into the ignition.

Amy, Helen and Patricia were shaken-up and nervous. Amy and Patricia's hands swept strands of their long hair away from their foreheads; their hair now hung down to their shoulders, having come undone during the fight. Orion and Gierek were also shaken up.

"You okay?" Orion asked the women.

"Do they look okay, arsehole?" Gierek yelled, his manner one of violent fury.

"I'm only asking!"

"We're shaken up, but okay," Amy responded. She dialed a number on her phone. "Come on, Captain, come on! Pick up your cell! Damn it! His cell's switched off! And we don't have the number for Dace Apartment!"

"We'll find it," Tony said.

"If we're lucky!" Dave added.

***

Captain Siffrey, Jeris Bridgeman, Harper Jones, Jake Chambers and Rudy Foxworth were with the two Cuban women, watching the waves of Biscayne Bay bombard the beach's golden-brown sand. The white stonework of Dace Apartment was ten yards behind them.

At that moment, two trucks raced either side of them, and bearded Cubans with flick-knives scrambled out of the back. The female informants screamed with horror before knives sped into their chests.

Both women fell to the sand, but Siffrey and the vice cops yanked their handguns out of their jacket pockets. With a barrage of lethal gunfire, Bridgeman and Jones dropped five Cubans whilst Chambers and Foxworth took down another five. His handgun blazing, Siffrey felled three brutes in six seconds, then turned to fire at two men from the truck behind. Two blasts dispatched one man before another three accounted for the second.

But the Cubans threw a hail of flick-knives, which viciously struck the bearded cops. Bridgeman, Jones, Chambers and Foxworth died as quickly and savagely as the informants, falling lifelessly to the sand.

Siffrey ran between the trucks into the apartment, but the mob leader took his handgun from his jacket pocket, aimed and fired toward the captain. The bullet slammed through Siffrey's shoulder blade, then through his chest. He fell, unconscious, in front of the apartment's steps.

A squad van skidded to a halt behind the two trucks, trapping the trucks between the van and the ocean, cutting off the mobsters' escape. Dave, Tony, Orion and Gierek along with Amy, Helen and Patricia scrambled out of the van and carried out their retribution before the Cubans could throw more knives. Only the mob leader had a handgun; Dave sent three gunshots into him so he hurtled to the beach. Tony cut down two guys with four shots whilst Orion brought down another two with five blasts and Gierek dropped three brutes with six rounds, all three alternating the direction of their gunfire by directing their fire from one Cuban to another.

As Amy's gunfire caught two mobsters in the chest and head and felled them, Helen and Patricia each blazed three blasts into two other thugs, the bullets slamming through one crook's solar plexus and the other's chest. All four brutes died instantly. The last two criminals threw two flick-knives toward Orion and Gierek, and the cops dodged aside.

Dave fired three shots into one Cuban, then five into another, and both bearded killers died in the next five or six seconds.

"The vice cops are dead!" Gierek cried.

"And the informants!" Orion shouted.

"Captain Siffrey is breathing," Tony said.

"Siffrey was hit in the shoulder blade and the upper chest," Dave said. "I'll use my hanky to stem the flow of blood!"

"I'll call an ambulance," Orion suggested.

"Get on it!" Gierek insisted.

***

At the café in Miami's Mount Sinai Hospital, Amy, Helen and Patricia were gulping large sips of coffee to calm their nerves. Amy and Patricia pulled from their purses thin white headbands to hold their hair well away from their foreheads and feminine faces. Patricia then tied her hair in a ponytail, but Amy left her dark hair draped behind her headband and down both sides of her face until it reached her narrow shoulders. She pulled out a lipstick and painted her lips, but tears rolled down the women's faces.

"It's okay, Amy, Patricia, it wasn't your fault," Helen assured them.

"It wasn't your fault either," Amy reassured her in return. "I just wish we'd got to Siffrey sooner."

"Stop, stop!" Patricia snapped. "Damn it, stop!"

"Siffrey wouldn't want us to cry like this," Helen begged Amy. "We brought down two ruthless mobs. And Siffrey would want us to be strong."

"Siffrey will make it," Patricia promised both women. "I know he will."

Then Officers Matt Cantrell, Matt Brogan and Andy Harmon entered the café and approached the women's table. Cantrell saw his wife, Amy, crying.

"You've taken this very badly, honey," he told her.

"You all have," Brogan remarked.

"Us men have taken it as badly as you ladies," Harmon said.

"I need your strong arms to comfort me," Amy told her husband, stammering feebly. She rose from her seat, fell between Matt

Cantrell's arms and chest and violently kissed him.

"Hey!" Cantrell exclaimed. "You are in a state, honey. It's all right."

"Brogan," Helen began. "Can I go on a date with you? Not tonight, because we're all having dinner at that Cuban restaurant in Little Havana. But maybe tomorrow or the next day?"

"And I fancy a date with you, Harmon," Patricia told Andy.

"This is a fine time for you ladies to think about dating men," Harmon retorted sarcastically.

"Knock it off, Andy," Brogan insisted. "Helen and I have felt the chemistry between us for a long time. And I know you and Patricia love each other. At least think about it."

"Okay, I'm in, Matt," Harmon agreed.

"Thanks, Harmon," Patricia said shyly.

"And thank you, Brogan," Helen said.

"Okay, guys," Amy cut in. "How about we join Bradley and Selma beside Siffrey's bed in Intensive Care? Are you ready?"

***

In the Intensive Care ward, Dave and Tony sat on one side of Siffrey's bed, John Orion and Eddie Gierek on the other.

"That mobster you interrogated in the car park," Orion said to Dave. "He said Siffrey sent you and Selma to the Bahamas to wire the mob's money through to Siffrey's bank account here in Miami. That's why these mobsters tried to knife us."

"Bradley and Selma never set foot in the Bahamas," Gierek objected. "And Siffrey had no way of gaining the mob's bank details or paperwork to make this possible. But Calvera and Batista sent those men to kill us with knives rather than rifles so the knives couldn't be traced back to Calvera and Batista."

"Chief Mills attacked and threatened both arms dealers with a.45 Magnum remember," Dave explained. "Under duress, they handed over their PIN numbers and bank details, Mills faked their signatures on written papers and sent a gang of dirty cops to the Bahamas to okay it with the bank in Nassau to wire the money through to a secret bank account here in Florida. The question is, where is this bank account?"

"There's something else," Tony suggested.

"Carry on."

"After embezzling the mob's money, Mills passed the buck by blaming Captain Siffrey and us two Feds. That's why Siffrey is lying in Intensive Care, four vice cops and two informants are dead and us four guys and three policewomen very nearly died in the car park. But we can't prove all this."

"The day is young," Dave decided. "I'll phone the city's SWAT team, and they can send two squads of heavily armed cops to hit Calvera's place opposite North Beach and Batista's place at Biscayne."

"I'll do that," Erikson declared, as he entered the ward with Cantrell, Brogan and Harmon.

Amy, Helen and Patricia were accompanying them, and Officer Dill followed behind.

"This is our jurisdiction, not yours," Cantrell told Dave.

"So, I have the authority," Erikson stated.

"Well, what are you waiting for?" Dave demanded.

Then Chief Mills made his way into the ward.

"How's Captain Siffrey?" he asked.

"What the fuck do you care?" Patricia yelled.

"It's okay, Hayes," Dill pleaded. "Just cool it."

"It's not okay!" Patricia shouted.

Helen glared at Mills. "You stole the mob's money and laundered it into a secret bank account where we can't find it!"

"You blamed Siffrey, Bradley and Selma for this crime!" Amy screamed. "So, two mobs tried to massacre us!"

"Get the fuck out of here now!" Erikson growled.

"You're talking to your commanding officer, not a motherfucker, punk!" Mills shouted with rage. "I could do you for slander, so your next journey is inside a prison van to death row!"

"It's not slander," Brogan said.

"The mob put a contract out on Siffrey, Bradley and Selma," Harmon snapped.

"After you embezzled their money into your bank account somewhere in Florida," Cantrell remarked.

"Tell us where your account is!" Gierek yelled.

"You have nothing on me!" Mills screamed.

"You're right, we have nothing," Tony told him.

"Except for one loose end," Dave said. "The location of the secret apartment where Captain Siffrey and the four vice cops were protecting two women informants was kept strictly confidential. The mob had no way of knowing it was called Dace Apartment on South Beach. Unless somebody on the inside phoned them. Neither Tony, myself nor the vice cops have Calvera or Batista's telephone or cell phone numbers, nor do we know their email addresses. Only you would have this knowledge, probably through criminal connections with the arms dealers."

"And when am I supposed to have made this tip-off call?" Mills challenged Dave.

"I don't know when, but I know you tipped off Calvera," Dave said. "When we foiled a mob attack in Miami PD's car park, Erikson's guys shot and killed all the mobsters except one, who was fatally injured. I interrogated the bastard, and he told me Captain Siffrey had sent Selma and myself to the Bahamas to wire the mob's money through to Siffrey's bank account here in Miami. Then the bastard died. Siffrey and us Feds had no bank details or forms to carry this out; we never set foot in the Bahamas, and if we checked Siffrey's bank account there would be no increase in money. You scared Calvera and Batista with a .45 Magnum, stole their forms and then sent money launderers to the Bahamas.

"God knows who these money launderers were, either dirty cops or internal affairs. But they laundered the arms dealers' three hundred million dollars into a secret bank account somewhere here in Florida. Your bank account.

"Another thing. Only a small circle of people knew about this embezzlement of drugs and arms money, and Siffrey wasn't one of them. We only found out from that fatally injured mobster I grilled in the car park. The only people who knew about you assaulting Calvera and Batista, stealing bank details and faking their signatures were these two arms dealers, the mob they control, and of course you, yourself, Mills. And the mysterious, unknown men you sent to the Bahamas to launder the three hundred million into another account here in Florida. Where is this bank account, Mills?"

"I've had enough of this garbage!" Mills yelled. "You will all face a charge of slander!"

He stormed out of the ward.

"We'll be damned if we ever allow ourselves to be scared of you," Orion shouted after him.

"Go back to your rathole where you came from!" Gierek called.

"This is not a matter of what we know, it's a matter of what we can prove," Erikson informed Dave and Tony. "At some point, both of you must take a flight and then a speedboat trip to Nassau in the Bahamas, drop in on that bank and ask questions about the transfer of that three hundred million from the arms dealers' offshore account. Trace this money to that secret account here in Florida. If this account is in the chief's name, we'll hang Mills for the rest of his life. I'm determined to see that son of a bitch rot on death row for corruption, money laundering, criminal connections to Florida's arms trafficking rings and the massacre of four vice cops and two informants at that apartment on South Beach. Hospital security will protect Captain Siffrey from reprisal attacks by the mob."

"Siffrey is safe for now," Cantrell decided. "About those SWAT teams hitting Calvera and Batista's estates?"

"I'll call the SWAT team commander now," Erikson replied.

***

On the opposite side of the highway from North Beach, a SWAT team closed in on

Calvera's estate. Leading this team were two strong, muscled men, one with long black hair, the other with short blond hair. Behind these guys were two Arab Americans with long hair and beards, a black-haired woman, and two blonde ladies, one with long hair and one with short hair. They were followed by a bald guy in his fifties, a man with long dark hair, another blonde woman and a well-muscled guy with long blond hair. Taking up the rear was a forty-eight-year-old man with thick hair.

The black-haired commander gave the signal, and the team bashed in the front door and stormed inside the building. But they trod on tripwires, which set off explosive devices.

The whole building was blown to pieces by five savage blasts, massacring the entire SWAT team, including the two strongly muscled commanders.

***

At Biscayne, the second SWAT team advanced stealthily toward Batista's estate. Leading them was a rugged man with long black hair and a woman with medium-length blonde hair. Behind these commanders was a tall, dark-haired woman, two bald black men, a bald white guy, and five youthful men, two of them black and three white. A young woman with short blonde hair came next, walking in front of another youthful woman with long blonde hair, and two white guys with short hair and beards. The rugged, long-haired commander gestured with his hand, and the team smashed their combined weight and strength against the front door, forcing it open. They hurried inside the building, but again their boots caught on tripwires, detonating explosive devices.

Four savage blasts erupted, demolishing the whole building and killing the entire SWAT team, including the two commanders.

***

The uniformed police arrived at both scenes of destruction, joined by the forensics and CSI teams. All the men and women were appalled by the carnage and loss of life in both explosions.

Dave and Tony attended both crime scenes, and then drove to the call center.

"Calvera and Batista escaped," Tony said.

"And somebody tipped them off the two SWAT teams were coming," Dave observed. "My finger points at Chief Mills."

"One way to find out," Tony said.

"Yeah? Tell me."

"We ferret through Florida's national phone line and trace any calls made from Mills' telephone and cell phone in the last two or three days and find out anything incriminating."

"Already on it. That's why I'm driving to the call center," Dave said.

Three minutes later, they arrived.

***

Inside the building's control room, Dave and Tony approached a thirty-six-year-old dark-haired man, seven other guys with short hair of various colors and two women in their early sixties, one gray-haired and the other blonde. The blonde lady was the call center's manager whilst the dark-haired man was a professional phone hacker who taught the other employees this skill.

"What can I do for you young men?" the blonde woman asked.

"This is police business," Dave told her. "We want to hack into Chief Gary Mills' telephone calls and cell calls he made in the last three days. We want you to trace Chief Mills and record conversations he's had with two arms dealers. Mills lives at number twenty-five in Little Havana. Luis Calvera lives opposite North Beach, and Ramon Batista lives in Biscayne. Or they did, before their properties were destroyed by explosive devices."

"We should search the whole of Miami and the rest of Florida for Calvera, Batista and their arms rings," Tony suggested.

"The cops don't know where to look," Dave replied. "It would be like looking for salt in a pot of stew. But something will come to the surface about their whereabouts."

Dave addressed the professional phone hacker. "Can you do a trace on Chief Mills' telephone and cell phone calls?"

"Your wish is my command, young man." The dark-haired man laughed.

"I'm older than you," Dave objected.

***

An hour later, Dave and Tony arrived back at Miami PD. They approached Squad Leader Erikson and Officers Cantrell, Brogan and Harmon.

"We've dug up more dirt on Chief Mills," Dave informed the vice cops.

"More dirt on Chief Mills?" Harmon asked.

"Tell us the not-so-pleasant news," Brogan said.

"Where did you go?" Harmon wanted to know.

"We're dying to hear this," Erikson told Dave.

The three long-haired men ran their hands through their beards.

Cantrell's hand swiped through his blond hair. "Come on, then," he demanded.

"Well," Dave began, "us Feds dropped in on the call center, ordered the people there to run a trace on Mills' phone, and unearthed something sinister. The first suspicious call was received on an airliner coming back from the Bahamas. There was background noise from the airplane's passengers talking loudly and the engines. We did not hear the voice of the man who replied, but either he was a dirty cop or some corrupt asshole from internal affairs. Probably one of the men Mills sent to the Bahamas to launder the mob's money into Mills' secret bank account. The second telephone call was to Calvera's property opposite North Beach. This call was made fourteen minutes before one mob attacked us with flick-knives in the car park and twenty-two minutes before the second mob attacked Dace Apartment on South Beach, killed those four vice cops and two women informants and shot Captain Siffrey.

"During this call, Mills told Calvera how Siffrey had confiscated the arms dealers' PIN numbers, bank details and forms from Mills and sent Selma and me to the Bahamas to launder the dealers' millions into Siffrey's account in Miami. Mills lied by claiming us two Feds wired this three hundred million bucks through, but if you check Siffrey's account, you'll know straight away the dollars haven't increased to a nine-figure number. Mills told Calvera we came in and out of Miami PD regularly, and he also told Calvera how Captain Siffrey and four vice cops were at Dace Apartment on South Beach. He gave an order to Calvera; he wanted Siffrey, Selma and me out of the way, and Calvera promised Mills two mobs were on their way, which resulted in those two attacks in the car park and outside Dace Apartment.

"Why does Mills want the three of us out of the way? In his first call to the man on the plane, he told this man we were becoming dangerous. Selma and I were apparently dangerous because we always smash cases wide open, we have brains and experience and we would smell corruption before you vice cops did. Calling Captain Siffrey a black bastard, Mills said he was dangerous because he was honest and could not be corrupted.

"One more point about this call to the man on the plane. Due to the background noise, I failed to pick up what this man was saying. Only three words: Money, wired and 'nando.'"

"Not nando," Tony realized. "Orlando, here in Florida. This anonymous individual, probably from internal affairs, told Mills the money had been wired through to his bank account in Orlando. The plane's background noise wiped out the rest of what this man said, but we heard Mills perfectly. He was calling from his address in Little Havana. Now we know where his secret bank account is, and at some point, we must take a trip there."

"Any more calls from that bastard?" Erikson asked.

"Two more calls," Dave said. "To Calvera and Batista. Shortly after we confronted Mills in the Intensive Care ward, he made two cell phone calls, warning them the SWAT teams would attack shortly. But two things about these mobile calls don't add up."

"Mills made those calls," Brogan said firmly.

"And like a top-quality camera…" Harmon cut in.

"…a phone trace never lies," Brogan finished.

"Give Bradley a chance," Erikson suggested.

Dave took back over. "You, Erikson, Cantrell and I only mentioned the SWAT teams' oncoming operations in the Intensive Care ward an hour before the SWAT teams hit Calvera and Batista's estates. Apart from the fact Mills wasn't present or even outside the ward to overhear our conversation, setting explosives throughout two estates is a long, delicate and dangerous task, which could not have been done in only an hour. And there is no record to suggest Calvera and Batista are explosives experts, so members of their arms ring must be. That's the first thing that doesn't add up."

"And the second thing?" Brogan asked.

"The second thing is the *actual* times Mills made those calls. 11 a.m. and 11:15 a.m., over six hours before the SWAT teams hit those two estates. Giving the mob six hours to set the booby traps. The SWAT teams hit those estates at 5:30 p.m., an hour after Erikson's call from the hospital at 4:30 p.m. Which means Mills knew in advance the SWAT teams would attack those estates, even before you phoned the SWAT team commander."

"Mills has a sixth sense," Erikson speculated. "He knew the SWAT teams were the people for the job of hitting those two estates."

"We could've chosen the Miami vice squad for these operations," Harmon pointed out.

"Or the Feds," Brogan remarked.

"But his experience in smashing arms rings, where the mobsters are more lethal due to storing more deadly weapons than pimps or drug dealers, taught him that the SWAT teams were better armed for this job," Erikson realized. "The SWAT teams being armed and body-armored like marines."

"Chief Mills was ahead of the game," Cantrell said.

"But before we have Mills arrested," Tony said. "We all need a long night's sleep. What's the time?"

"It's 7 p.m. by my watch," Dave replied. "Me and Tony will sleep in the FBI's Florida headquarters."

"My vice squad arranged to have dinner at that Cuban restaurant in Little Havana," Erikson said. "Aren't you two interested?"

"And we promised to meet the others there at seven," Cantrell told Erikson. "We'd better set off now."

"You coming?" Erikson asked the Feds.

"No, we're too tired," Dave said.

"Another time," Tony suggested.

***

At Little Havana's Cuban restaurant, all ten vice cops were deep in conversation.

"It's bad enough Mills has criminal connections to arms rings," Orion complained.

"And other criminal syndicates too," Gierek added.

"Like prostitution rings and drug rings," Erikson said.

"But he's behind those two mob attacks against seven of us in the car park and Captain Siffrey's team at Dace Apartment," Amy said.

"Which put Siffrey in Mount Sinai Hospital," Helen snapped.

"What about those four incriminating phone calls?" Patricia asked. "The last two resulted in the massacres of two SWAT teams."

"Two teams who are hard to replace," Brogan growled.

"What do you suggest we do?" Harmon asked. "Have him arrested and tried so he goes down for life on death row?"

"That's too easy on Mills," Erikson told them. "We kill him."

"Are you serious?" Gierek asked.

"I am. He lives across the street," Erikson added.

***

At the FBI headquarters, Dave and Tony were fast asleep when three Feds approached them: Agents Robert Hook, Richard Brown and Jeris Bragan. All these men needed haircuts, their hair grown long after several months carrying out undercover work. Chief Robert Hook, head of the FBI's Florida branch, was overweight and had a bald patch between two sides of hair hanging down to his cheeks. He was in his late forties. Richard Brown was in his late thirties and had reddish-brown hair and a boyish face. Jeris Bragan was in his early forties with brown hair turning gray and a rugged face. They shook Dave and Tony awake.

"Cut it out!" Dave said.

"What is it?" Tony asked.

"Some bad news," Hook said.

"And it's really bad," Brown said.

"Want to hear it, guys?" Bragan asked.

"Enlighten us," Tony suggested.

"Chief Gary Mills is dead," Hook told them. "He was found at his place, number twenty-five in Little Havana, shot to death with a handgun. He was sat in his armchair when the attack happened."

"Oh my God!" Dave exclaimed.

"Who discovered his body?" Tony wanted to know.

"Miles Erikson's ten-strong team of vice cops," Brown said.

"You want us to drive you to the crime scene?" Hook asked. "The forensics and CSI teams are already there."

"No, Tony and I will go alone," Dave said. "Just the two of us."

"We'd better set off," Tony added.

***

Dave and Tony entered number twenty-five to encounter a grisly scene. Chief Mills was lying slumped in his armchair, his body riddled with bloody bullet wounds. Dave also noticed joy on the vice cops' faces in their relief that Mills was dead.

He approached the ten vice cops, with a pen ready to take down notes.

"None of you seem upset or traumatized by the chief's death," he said.

"We're not," Erikson replied.

"He will not be missed," Brogan said.

"He was scum," Harmon added.

"America is a better place without him," Cantrell remarked.

"None of us liked him," Dave replied.

"But no murder makes America a better place," Tony informed them. "Especially a rough state like Florida."

"You must come down to the department with us," Dave ordered.

"Ready when you are," Erikson said. "Officers Dill, Orion, Gierek, Amy Cantrell, Post and Hayes, we're needed down at Miami PD."

"We got that," Patricia responded.

"Let's go," Amy said.

***

At Miami PD, they interrogated the ten officers separately, with Dave interviewing five and Tony the other five. Dave's first suspect was Squad Leader Miles Erikson.

"I know you and your team were behind Chief Mills' death," Dave began.

"What makes you so sure?" Erikson asked.

"It's not just a hunch. When Tony and I arrived at the crime scene, you were all calm to the point of being smug and arrogant. Your eyes were smiling even if your mouths weren't. But even more concrete—the gunshot wounds on Chief Mills' body were still fresh and the blood was still wet and sticky. Meaning he had only been dead for an hour or two. The time now is 11 p.m. Chief Mills died round about 9 p.m. Not only was the blood still wet, but there were two other factors that cast doubt on your innocence."

"Fill me in."

"Your vice squad arrived at the Cuban restaurant in Little Havana round about 7 p.m., and you, Brogan, Harmon and Cantrell shortly afterward," Dave said. "In my experience, most Americans don't spend more than one and a half, maybe two hours at a restaurant. Don't lie to me, because I'll question the restaurant's bartender about how long you had to wait for your meals. Did your meals arrive after half an hour or an hour?"

"They arrived after forty minutes. At 7:50 p.m."

"Did you and your officers have desserts?" Dave asked.

"No," Erikson told him. "Only fruits. Guavas, mangoes and bananas imported straight from Cuba and Puerto Rico."

"And if it takes no more than twenty minutes to eat that…" Dave said. "You would've finished eating at ten past eight. Chief Mills' place is only across the road from the Cuban restaurant. The time period between 8:10 p.m. and 9 p.m. is fifty minutes. You should've all gone home and slept for the night. Not spent fifty minutes in and around the same district of Miami, unless you were planning something. Like retribution against Mills, which resulted in murder."

"Well, that's just supposition on your part," Erikson objected.

"Time is the first factor," Dave replied. "The second factor is the type of weapon used to kill Mills. The shell casings on the floor were from a handgun or revolver. If arms dealers like Calvera and Batista wanted to shoot somebody, being proficient in using more powerful, terrifying weapons, they or their mob would've used rifles or automatic weapons, or maybe a bomb, a grenade or a rocket launcher. Dextor Boyd's men who attacked us on that beach and downed that FBI plane used a rocket launcher and rifles. The store raiders that attacked Tony Selma and Nathan Dill's vice squad at that liquor store used rifles. The two SWAT teams at Calvera and Batista's estates were massacred by booby traps set off by tripwires. Drug dealers and pimps often use handguns to kill people. But arms dealers prefer more fearsome weapons.

"All of you carry handguns and revolvers, but only one of you committed the murder. Tony and I will interrogate all your officers to find any inconsistencies in your stories. Because Chief Mills was ruthless, brutal and corrupt, only his killer will do time, and only five years with less time due to parole. But if you and your officers keep lying, this will increase your time."

"We have nothing to hide," Erikson objected. "I told you what I told the forensics and CSI teams. We found Mills' body at 9 p.m. He must've been murdered shortly before we arrived."

"After the interrogations," Dave said, "you and your officers must hand your handguns and revolvers in to the forensics lab so we can do a ballistics report."

"Why didn't you conform to protocol and confiscate our weapons before the interrogations?" Erikson asked.

"I had no evidence to prove or even suggest your guilt. Only a hunch."

After more than two hours of interrogations, Dave and Tony found no inconsistencies in the officers' statements. The vice cops placed their handguns and revolvers inside evidence bags labeled with their names, and Dave and Tony carried all ten bags with twenty weapons to the forensics lab.

"All of them gave exactly the same story," Tony told Dave. "They arrived at number twenty-five at 9 p.m. They found Chief Gary Mills already dead. Nobody's story changed and there were no inconsistencies in their statements. Do you think it might've been a mob hit? By arms dealers or drug dealers? Or a burglary turned bad?"

"That's possible, but highly improbable," Dave said. "The arms dealers we're up against don't kill people with handguns. Their main weapons are rifles. But in an hour's time, the ballistics report and the bullets taken from Chief Mills' body will reveal whose gun killed Mills."

"With Captain Siffrey in hospital," Tony said, "who will run Miami PD in his absence?"

"Lieutenants Ken Ross and Alex Smith," Dave informed the young man. "The head of the FBI's Florida branch, Chief Robert Hook, will have contacted Ross and Smith to brief them about Mills' murder, and they'll arrive at the department shortly. When we've handed these weapons over to Forensics, we'll interview the bartender at the Cuban restaurant in Little Havana and then pay another visit to the crime scene. See if any new evidence comes up."

They entered the forensics lab through a very strong fire door with a glass window. They met four bearded men from the CSI team, three of them black and the fourth white. These men were tall, their sizeable muscles showing through their lab uniforms.

"Hi there," the bearded white guy greeted the Feds. "I'm Lee Houston, and I run this joint, the forensics and CSI Teams. My three assistants are Tom Cornelli, Robert Watts and Rick Jackson. Just call them Cornelli,

Watts and Jackson. And call me Houston. But you're rather late with handing in those twenty handguns. Why the delay?"

"These handguns belong to the men and women from Vice," Dave replied. "All of them, including Squad Leader Miles Erikson, are suspects in Chief Mills' murder. Apart from supposition or a hunch, I had no evidence to prove their guilt. Agent Selma and I interviewed all ten officers, but their stories were all the same. They all claim they found Mills shot to death in his armchair at 9 p.m., which I estimate as the time the murder happened. The weapons are here now."

"The time of death was 8:40 p.m.," Houston told him. "The bullets in Mills' body and the shell casings came from a .38 automatic handgun or automatic revolver."

"Each of the vice cops owns a handgun and an automatic revolver," Jackson said.

"By the shape of the casings, it was definitely an automatic revolver," Watts explained.

"That narrows the murder weapon down to ten revolvers in those evidence bags," Cornelli said. "We can rule out the ten handguns."

"All it takes now is to match the shell casings to one of the revolvers, and we have our killer," Houston said. "Not to mention DNA samples from the shell casings."

"We've already tried to extract DNA from the casings," Cornelli pointed out.

"And there was no DNA on the casings or the bullets we removed from Mills's body," Watts added. "But we found wool fibers on the bullets and the casings, meaning the killer wore thin woolen gloves."

"The killer was a professional assassin, a hitman," Cornelli told Houston.

"But it never snows in Florida," Houston continued. "Not even in the winter or at Christmas."

"In a hot climate, the killer's hands would sweat," Tony realized. "Did you extract DNA from the sweat passing through the gloves?"

"No, Agent Selma," Houston replied. "Due to padding underneath the wool covering on the killer's gloves, no sweat passed through the padding onto the wool, so the wool fibers on the bullets and the casings had no sweat or any other DNA."

"In that case," Dave said, "forget DNA and fingerprints. Just match the shell casings to one of the revolvers in the evidence bags. Tony and I will find out which of the vice cops owns woolen gloves."

"You're on," Houston said.

***

Dave and Tony were with Lieutenants Ken Ross and Alex Smith in the department's main office.

"We're taking over from Captain Siffrey as senior officers at Miami PD," Ross said.

"At least until Siffrey recovers from his coma," Smith added.

"We got that," Dave said.

"You both have an update on the Gary Mills murder case?" Ross asked.

"Not much," Dave said. "Because all ten vice cops hated Mills with a passion, any one of them could've fired the shots that killed him. Forensics are trying to match the shell casings to one of the ten revolvers which was the gun that fired the fatal shots. Five shots assassinated Chief Mills."

"So, it was an automatic revolver, not a handgun that killed him?" Smith asked.

"The shell casings from the crime scene and the five bullets removed from Mills's body were from an automatic revolver," Dave confirmed.

"What else?" Ross snapped.

"Fibers from woolen gloves were found on the casings and the bullets, but because the gloves had strong padding underneath the wool, no sweat or DNA from the killer's hands passed through the wool onto the casings or the bullets."

"The casings will be matched to the weapon that killed Mills," Tony told Ross. "We must search the vice cops for woolen gloves, and this will hang the killer. Very few people in a hot climate like Florida wear woolen gloves, not even in the winter."

"You have your fingers pointed at the people from Vice?" Ross asked.

"For a number of reasons," Dave replied. "Reason number one is when we arrived at Number twenty-five in Little Havana, their eyes were smiling as if they were happy to the point of being smug and arrogant that Mills perished. Usually, people who discover a dead body are shocked and traumatized, but everybody was calm, which draws our suspicions to these men and women. Reason number two: although I estimated the time of Mills' death to be about 9 p.m., the pathologist discovered he died at 8:40 p.m. The vice cops were eating dinner out at the Cuban restaurant nearby between 7:50 p.m.

and 8:10 p.m., after waiting forty minutes for their food orders to arrive at their table. After 8:10 p.m., they should've paid the bill and driven home, but there was a fifty-minute gap until they claim they visited Mills at 9 p.m. and discovered him dead with five gunshots inside him. During those fifty minutes, they could've been planning to kill him, but they took less time. Mills died at 8:40 p.m., meaning the vice squad only spent thirty minutes planning his murder. They waited for twenty minutes before phoning Florida's FBI headquarters at 9 p.m. to tell the Feds, including myself and Agent Selma, they discovered Mills shot to death in his armchair.

"And reason number three for suspecting the vice squad is that an automatic revolver was used to kill Chief Mills. The mobsters in Calvera and Batista's arms rings don't use handguns or revolvers. They use rifles and, in two recent attacks on seven of us cops in the department's car park and on Siffrey's four vice cops and two women informants at Dace Apartment on South Beach, flick-knives, which cannot be traced back to Calvera and Batista the way rifles can. The use of a revolver in Chief Mills's assassination does not fit the MO of Calvera's arms ring. Unless Calvera and Batista got clever and tried to frame the vice cops by sending mobsters armed with revolvers to break into Chief Mills' place and murder Mills using a revolver."

"Which is highly unlikely," Tony objected. "The vice cops' identities and movements are kept strictly confidential. The mob would have no knowledge of who the vice cops are, let alone the fact they happened to be eating in a Cuban restaurant in Little Havana. Nobody in this department or in the vice squad discussed dinner out at this restaurant within earshot of potential criminals due to rules about careless talk. It would be pure coincidence if Calvera's men happened to break into Mills' place while the vice cops were eating in the Cuban restaurant opposite. More likely, they would try to frame Dave Bradley and me by using revolvers, for the mob know more about us two Feds than the vice cops. One mob has already attacked me, Dave and five of the vice squad in the car park, but with assistance from Erikson's guys, we killed all these mobsters. Another attack put Captain Siffrey in hospital because Mills stole the mob's money, embezzled it into a secret bank account, then phoned Calvera and blamed this money laundering on Siffrey, Dave and me. Like Mills, the mob wants us two Feds out of the way and may have framed us for Mills' murder by using revolvers, five taps to the chest."

"But it's extremely unlikely," Dave said.

"But if Mills tried to get you Feds and Siffrey killed," Ross said, "he deserved to die."

"Whoever killed him," Smith remarked. "Good luck to them."

"We must still bring the killers to justice," Dave told both men. "When we return from another trip to the crime scene, we'll find out from Forensics what the ballistics report says. Before we leave, we'll search the vice cops' leather jackets for the woolen gloves that left those wool fibers on the bullets and shell casings."

"I'll give you the go-ahead," Ross decided. "Get on with it."

***

Having found no trace of the woolen gloves inside the ten leather jackets, Dave and Tony drove to Little Havana. Tony bleeped Lee Houston, who answered on his cell phone.

"Hi there, Lee Houston here. Can I help you?"

"It's Agent Tony Selma. I need two favors. Can you send CSI Officers Cornelli, Watts and Jackson back down to number twenty-five in Little Havana? With ultraviolet lights to detect somebody else's DNA or fingerprints, or shoeprints in the carpet where other intruders may have entered the premises, one of them being Chief Mills' killer. And also check for tire marks outside the property where the intruders' vehicle may have pulled up in front before they got out."

"I'll send them down right away," Houston responded. "That's the first favor. What's the second?"

"To answer a question on the ballistics report and any new evidence you picked up about the murder. Has anything new come up?"

"Yeah, it has. The bullets and shell casings cannot be matched to any of the ten automatic revolvers. All these revolvers have been reloaded since the vice cops fired these revolvers at the two mobs who carried out those two attacks in the car park and at Dace Apartment on South Beach. Not one bullet is missing from any revolver, let alone five rounds. This proves not a single one of the cops' weapons was used to kill Mills, which casts doubt on their guilt. Lieutenants Ross and Smith reported to me that you found no woolen gloves in the pockets of their leather jackets?"

"That's correct," Tony told Houston. "But if one of Erikson's men or women did fire the fatal shots that killed Mills, he or she probably dumped the gloves along with the murder weapon into a garbage can.

"Another thing. If the killer wore gloves, we can't test the cops' hands for gunpowder residue, for any residue from the murder weapon would've seeped into the gloves, not the killer's hands. Just like we won't find DNA on the weapon or the shell casings.

"As soon as Agent Bradley and I have interviewed the bartender at the Cuban restaurant and the three CSI officers have detected shoeprints and tire marks at the crime scene, we must trace the tire marks to any possible store or gas station any possible intruders may have pulled up outside either before or after stopping off at the crime scene. And interview the guys who own this store or gas station. I also suggest Erikson and his vice cops perform lic detector tests, which will expose their guilt or innocence."

"I got that," Houston replied. "Anything else?"

"That's all," Tony said. "Goodbye."

The conversation ended, and Tony rearranged his glasses before scratching his mustache.

Dave rubbed his beard thoughtfully. "I owe Erikson's vice cops an apology."

"For what?" Tony asked.

"We put them through ten rigorous interrogations when they're probably innocent," Dave told him. "The bullets and shell casings couldn't be matched to any of the ten revolvers they own. And the weapons were reloaded after those two knife attacks in the car park and at Dace Apartment, but no bullets were missing. Not one, let alone five. Maybe Erikson's people were telling the truth, that they visited the property at 9 p.m. and found Mills dead on the premises, twenty minutes after the autopsy rules that he died. If we can't test their hands for gunpowder residue, then maybe lie detector tests will be our last chance to prove the guilt or innocence of these men and women. And now, we're at number twenty-five."

Dave stopped the car and turned off the ignition before he and Tony left the vehicle.

They walked down the road, tracing tire marks from a heavy vehicle leading around the street corner and then down the street past the Cuban restaurant.

"By the look of the tire marks," Dave observed, "a large, heavy vehicle, either a lorry or a truck, came round the corner, drove and stopped here before driving on past the Cuban restaurant behind us, on the opposite side of the street."

Dave turned to face the restaurant and saw CCTV cameras on the roof. "CCTV cameras," he said. "They'll give us a new lead."

"I have a hunch about what the truck was doing on that street just around the corner," Tony said.

"Go on."

"There's a fabric store three hundred yards down that street. They make really strong materials, including wool. Maybe they sell woolen gloves."

"You want to check it out?"

"Do you think it's a long shot?" Tony asked. "Several clothes stores and fabrics stores in Florida sell woolen gloves. But I'd better check it out."

"Wait until the three CSI officers arrive," Dave insisted.

"Why wait for them?"

"We'll all work together. The forensics and CSI officers will comb the property for shoeprints. Whilst they take time over this, I'll interview the bartender at the Cuban restaurant and check video footage from those cameras, and you'll interview the people in that fabric store. You got that?"

"I got it," Tony replied.

At that moment, a van halted in front of Dave's car, and CSI officers Tom Cornelli, Robert Watts and Rick Jackson emerged from the vehicle. Carrying an ultraviolet light, they approached Dave and Tony.

"Thanks for coming," Dave said.

"Hi there, guys," Cornelli, Watts and Jackson replied seriously.

"This better be good," Cornelli said.

"It will be," Dave replied.

"This ultraviolet light might turn up something we missed," Jackson said. "Like shoeprints that shouldn't be on the property. Let's jump to it, guys."

The CSI detectives conducted another examination of Mills' place, and their ultraviolet light exposed the ten sets of shoeprints from the vice cops, but also two other sets of shoeprints that seemed to be left by sneakers.

"The vice cops made these shoeprints," Jackson observed.

"But two other sets of shoeprints from pairs of sneakers lead around the house," Cornelli said. "And they roughed up the carpet, going left, right and center as if there was a fight."

"Mills put up a fight, but was outnumbered two to one," Watts said. "Mills was a big, strong man, but his two attackers were just as big."

"They pushed him violently into the armchair," Cornelli continued. "One of them pulled out his revolver and popped him with five taps to the chest."

"The front door was intact," Jackson told the other CSI men. "There was no sign of forced entry."

"Meaning one thing," Watts pointed out.

"You tell us," Cornelli prompted.

"'They rang the doorbell, and Mills answered the door," Watts said. "Then they pushed him through the hallway into the dining room and there was a fight, but no punches were thrown."

"Because there were no bruises to Mills's face, no blood on his beard and no defensive wounds on his hands," Jackson speculated. "The two attackers quickly restrained him, threw him with violent force into the armchair and one of them popped him with his revolver. The scuff marks on the carpet were made by sneakers, but another thing."

"Spill the beans," Cornelli said.

"The ultraviolet light has not only detected shoeprints left by sneakers, but also traces of floor cleaner, and the smell is still very strong. Carpet cleaner that smells of chemicals and mushrooms. Strong mushrooms."

"Two other clues." Watts nodded.

"After one of the attackers popped Chief Mills," Cornelli pointed out, "they opened Mills' safe and stole all his money, to make it look like a robbery gone bad. They used his keys."

"But it wasn't thieves or burglars who pulled the hit," Jackson said.

"The arms ring sanctioned the hit," Watts concluded. "Or Calvera and Batista did. There are large strides between the two sets of footprints. The two killers were big guys— tall, strong guys with long legs that could walk a bigger stride."

"If Mills had been standing when he was shot," Cornelli remarked, "we could tell by the angle the bullets hit and traveled through his body how tall the guy who fired the gun was."

"But Mills was slumped into the armchair when the guy popped him," Watts said. "There's nothing to tell whether the killer was a man or a woman. One of the seven men or three women in the vice squad."

"But now we know two men carried out the hit," Cornelli informed both detectives.

"And there could've been more men waiting outside, men from the truck that left those tire marks," Jackson said.

"What else?" Watts asked.

"Nothing else," Cornelli said. "Only we need to find out which store happened to be cleaning its carpets with floor cleaner smelling of mushrooms."

"One other thing," Jackson observed. "As both killers fought with and restrained Mills, no DNA came off their hands, faces or hair. Because they were wearing gloves and balaclavas."

"We may get more info from Agent Bradley regarding what the Cuban restaurant's CCTV cameras picked up," Cornelli said.

***

In the restaurant, Dave questioned a middle-aged Cuban woman, who was the manager and bartender.

"You overheard the conversation between the ten vice cops having dinner around that table?" Dave asked.

"Si, señor, I did."

"Did any other staff overhear the conversation?"

"They were in the kitchen passing orders to the cooks," the woman informed him. "Only I was in the restaurant area behind the bar. The guy called Erikson said something incriminating, which means these men and women killed Chief Gary Mills."

"What did they say, and what did he say?" Dave asked.

"They were discussing those two knife attacks in Miami PD's car park and an apartment on South Beach, then two estates belonging to two arms dealers being destroyed by booby traps, massacring two SWAT teams," the woman told him. "And four incriminating phone calls made by Chief Mills to the arms dealers behind these brutal crimes. A bearded guy with glasses named Brogan said these SWAT teams were hard to replace. Another bearded guy named Harmon asked the third bearded guy, Erikson, 'What do you suggest we do? Have him arrested and tried so he goes down for life on death row?'

Erikson told him the really incriminating part: 'That's too easy on Mills. We kill him.' Another clean-shaven man with long gray hair named Gierek asked, 'Are you serious?' And Erikson replied, 'I am. He lives across the street.' Then the waiters and waitresses delivered the cops' meals."

"At what time?" Dave said.

"7:50 p.m."

"Did they have desserts afterward?" Dave asked.

"Only fruit," the woman remarked. "I can't remember which fruits."

"An autopsy on Chief Mills' body ruled that he died round about 8:40 p.m.," Dave said. "Did you see the cops leaving round about that time, or knocking on Mills' front door? If not, did you hear any shots? Five shots from an automatic revolver?"

"No, Detective Bradley," the woman replied. "I was in the kitchen with the waiters and cooks reporting a complaint from one of the customers. The man said his pizza was too cold. It was a Cuban pizza. I had the pizza reheated in the oven before returning it to the guy's table, and there were no more complaints. I'm convinced those ten cops killed Chief Mills."

"One piece of concrete evidence will prove or disprove this," Dave said. "You have three CCTV cameras on the roof of your restaurant. You mind if I study video camera footage of who was outside the chief's place at 8:40 p.m., knocked on his front door and forced their way onto his premises?"

"You carry on," the woman agreed. "I'll show you which room upstairs the video cameras are in."

"Thanks, señora."

She opened the door behind the bar and led him upstairs, where she showed him the video camera footage. He saw a large truck come round the street corner and mount the pavement. Two bearded men were in the front seats, one bald and the other with long hair. Coming out of the truck's main compartment through the back were four menacing bearded guys: two Cubans with long hair, one of them wearing glasses, and two white Americans with beards, one with long, reddish-brown hair and the other bald. All six men were carrying powerful, high-velocity rifles. But the last two guys could not be identified: they were wearing gloves on their hands and balaclavas over their heads. Both were tall and well built.

"Six guys altogether, four Americans and two Cubans, all bearded men," Dave observed. "They're carrying rifles. But those two guys are wearing sneakers, jeans and probably shirts with leather jackets over the top. And balaclavas over their heads and woolen gloves on their hands. They were well-covered to prevent any traces of their DNA being left on the floor and furniture and Mills himself when they restrained him, threw him into his armchair and popped him. Where the other six men were carrying rifles, these two guys carried automatic revolvers. The revolvers that killed Chief Mills. Can we show this footage on the news, señora?"

***

Down the street just around the corner from Little Havana, Tony made his way inside the fabric store. He was greeted by a young Puerto Rican woman.

"Can I help you, señor?" the woman asked.

"Si, señorita." Tony chuckled. "I'm FBI. Federal Agent Tony Selma. Can I ask some questions?"

"Go right ahead."

"Have you recently sold woolen gloves to a gang of men?" Tony asked. "Were they

Cubans, Puerto Ricans or Americans? Can you describe their physical appearances, and were they driving a large truck? What shoes were they wearing, were they smartly dressed or casually dressed, and have you cleaned your carpet with floor cleaner that smells of strong mushrooms? The smell from your carpet is very pungent."

"I have cleaned my carpet with floor cleaner smelling of mushrooms," the woman replied. "I sold two packets of woolen gloves to one of the men, and then they left the store and the guy I sold the gloves to called out to two guys who'd stayed in the back of the truck whilst the other six guys were inside my store."

"There were six of them!" Tony exclaimed. "And two in the back of the truck."

"Si, señor."

"Can you describe these six guys?"

"Four were white Americans and two were Cubans," the woman recounted. "I didn't get a look at the two men in the truck's main compartment. But the six men who came in here, all were bearded men. Two Americans and two Cubans had long hair, one of the Cubans being an evil-looking guy with glasses. All these guys looked evil and brutal. The other two bearded Americans had bald heads. They were all of medium height, slim and muscular. They wore khaki trousers, formal shirts, and leather jackets over the top. But they wore sneakers, not shoes."

"They wore sneakers?" Tony confirmed her statement. "And the floor cleaner would've soaked their sneakers. Do you have CCTV footage of the men in the shop and inside the truck?"

"Si, señor," the woman replied. "I'll show you."

In the back room, the CCTV camera footage showed the six men inside the shop, and the Cuban with glasses buying the two sets of woolen gloves. Then two other men wearing balaclavas jumped out of the back of the truck, walked through the open door into the store and browsed around. The woman glanced round at the masked men as the six guys stared with intimidating eyes toward her. She kept quiet, and the gloves were passed to the two masked men before all eight brutes left. The men jumped into the truck, and the large vehicle continued its route to Little Havana.

Tony turned to the woman.

"You must've been really terrified," he said. "I'm sorry you went through that. But we will catch these men and put them behind bars. You don't have to lie by telling me those two masked men did not enter the store and stayed in the back of the truck. These masked men murdered a high-ranking police officer. But because they entered your store, the floor cleaner on your carpet would've soaked their sneakers and would be detected at the crime scene. The two pairs of gloves they bought were used to stop their DNA passing onto the crime scene, and their balaclavas hid their identities. But you don't have to be scared. We will catch this gang. Can we use this CCTV footage as evidence in a court case?"

"You must be crazy!" the woman snapped. "And spend the rest of my life looking over my shoulder? The answer is no!"

"Okay, okay," Tony agreed. "We can use other footage from CCTV cameras at Little Havana. Thank you for your time."

***

Inside the Cuban Restaurant, Dave was still with the bartender watching the CCTV footage.

"The two masked men knock on Mills' door at 8:40 p.m.," he observed. "Mills opens the door; the men grab him in restraint holds and manhandle him into the dining room. The door is still open. But Miles Erikson's vice squad would've seen all this from the restaurant. Why didn't they intervene and take on the gang of men?" Dave glanced back toward the Cuban woman.

"When the ten men and women from Vice paid the bill at 8:20 p.m.," the woman said. "They left the restaurant and walked up Little Havana, planning retribution against Chief Mills."

"Did they go west or did they go east?" Dave asked. "Because the truck carrying the gang of armed men came from that street northwest of this restaurant. If the vice cops had been heading west, they would've noticed the truck coming and stopping outside the chief's property."

"They made their way east," the woman told him. "And the truck drove into this street twenty minutes later at 8:40 p.m. I'll run the footage back to 8:20 p.m., when these cops left the restaurant."

She replayed the camera footage from that time. In the footage, the vice cops were leaving the restaurant and making their way in the direction opposite the street where the truck came from.

Dave turned to the bartender. "You were convinced Miles Erikson's vice cops murdered Chief Mills because of their incriminating conversation. And I'm convinced they would've done it and were walking down the street planning his assassination. But the arms dealers in the truck got to Mills before Erikson's vice cops did. We'll need to record the truck's license plate and record all this as evidence to clear the cops' names. Can we use this footage, or at least use your printer to take photographs of what happened?"

"Si, Agent Bradley," the woman agreed. "I'm sorry I suspected these cops."

"I suspected them, too," Dave remarked.

***

Dave and Tony entered Chief Mills' place, Dave carrying the photos of the truck, its license plate and the gang of armed men.

"These photos will clear the cops' names," he said.

"And hang those eight armed men," Tony said.

Both FBI agents exchanged information with Cornelli, Watts and Jackson about what they had uncovered during their investigations.

"The vice cops will be performing lie detector tests now," Dave told everybody.

***

Having driven to the FBI headquarters, the vice cops entered the building and greeted Chief Hook and Agents Brown and Bragan. With the three Feds was a mixed-race man with a Mexican-style mustache who was aged thirty-three. His name was Damien Woodward, and he was an expert on lie detectors.

"You've all come here for the polygraph tests?" Damien asked.

"We have," Erikson replied.

He, Cantrell, Brogan and Harmon along with Orion, Gierek and Dill seemed positive going in to the tests. Helen was smiling, as were Amy and Patricia; their eyes were sharp and their foreheads creased up. They sat on the bench outside the interrogation room. Erikson was the first cop to enter and begin the lie detector test.

The ten tests took three hours and twenty minutes, and all ten officers passed. Afterward, Helen Post and Matt Brogan had a night out eating dinner at a health food restaurant. Brogan was dressed in a black suit while Helen wore a suit consisting of a medium-length blue skirt and a purple blazer.

"We passed all ten tests," Helen enthused. "I must admit I was nervous."

"I was, too," Brogan told her. "Only a fool wouldn't be."

"Our food is coming," Helen remarked.

After returning from the restaurant, Brogan and Helen drove up Brogan's driveway and stopped the car. Brogan switched off the ignition and they vacated the vehicle. Still dressed in their suits, their mouths met.

"I've thought of something," Brogan said.

"You've forgotten something very important," Helen chuckled. Her feminine face brightened up with a grin.

"How did you know?" Brogan snapped with surprise.

"I just know. And I also know what it is you've forgotten. The white wine."

"You're sharp."

Helen laughed. "And you're hot."

Then they heard footsteps.

"Who's that?" Brogan asked.

"CSI detectives Jackson, Watts and Cornelli," Jackson announced.

"Are we under arrest again?" Helen asked sarcastically.

"No," Jackson said. "Dave and Tony sent us over here to apologize on their behalf for accusing both of you and Erikson's people of Chief Mills's murder."

"They weren't brave enough to come over here themselves," Helen retorted. "So they sent you."

"They're busy apologizing to Matt and Amy Cantrell, and Andy Harmon and Patricia Hayes," Cornelli replied.

"So they sent us," Watts told the young couple.

"Detective Houston and Lieutenants Ross and Smith are passing on their regrets to Squad Leader Erikson and to Officers Orion, Gierek and Dill, as well as Dave's regrets," Cornelli explained.

"Can you thank Dave and Tony for their apologies on our behalf?" Brogan asked.

"We will," Jackson said.

"Aren't you forgetting something, Matt?" Helen added.

"Oh yeah, the wine," Brogan replied.

✳✳✳

Andy Harmon and Patricia Hayes were eating at Andy's place.

The doorbell rang.

"I'll get that." Harmon rose from his chair, approached the front door and opened it.

Tony was at the door. "Hi there."

"Hi, Tony."

"And I repeat the word hi," Patricia added. "You owe us both an apology."

"Not to mention an apology from Dave," Harmon said.

"That's why I'm here," Tony told them. "Dave deeply regrets accusing you and the whole of Erikson's vice squad of Chief Mills's murder."

"How does he know we're innocent?" Patricia said.

"Apart from all ten of us passing ten lie detector tests," Harmon pointed out.

"CCTV footage showed you all leaving the Cuban restaurant and walking in the opposite direction from Gary Mills's place," Tony replied. "And then, a truck with eight armed men stopped outside Mills's place, and whilst six men waited outside, two men wearing balaclavas broke in, restrained him, threw him into his armchair and shot him.

That was twenty minutes after you left the restaurant. After the killers left the crime scene, CCTV footage showed the ten of you heading for Mills's place, making your way inside and finding Mills dead. We know you're all innocent, and Dave apologizes for suspecting you. My apology is just as sincere."

"Thanks for coming all the way here to tell us," Harmon said.

"No hard feelings, toward either of you," Patricia promised Tony. "You want to drop in for a coffee or a beer?"

"No thanks," Tony replied. "I'll be on my way. Good day."

"Good day."

***

Matt and Amy Cantrell were eating pizza and sipping glasses of lemonade. Amy's hair was loose, hanging down to her shoulders. Then the Emily Blunt lookalike heard the doorbell.

"You hear that?" she asked Matt.

"I heard it," he said. "I'll get it."

He rose from the settee and approached the front door, with Amy following behind. He opened the door, and Dave was on the other side.

"Hi there," Dave said.

"Hi, Bradley," Matt replied.

"I owe you both an apology," Dave informed them. "For accusing both of you of complicity in Chief Gary Mills's murder. What Tony and I implied was unforgivable. Tony has apologized on my behalf to Harmon and Hayes, and the three CSI detectives have apologized to Brogan and Post. The two lieutenants and CSI Officer Houston have passed on their regrets to Erikson, Orion, Gierek and Dill."

"Apology accepted," Matt told him.

"We don't bear any grudges," Amy reassured him.

"But one thing," Matt said. "How do you Feds know we're innocent? It's open to question whether or not lie detectors are foolproof."

"I'll show you the CCTV footage from the Cuban Restaurant in the morning," Dave promised him.

"Before you go," Amy added. "You want some pizza or lemonade?"

"I'm thirsty." Dave chuckled. "No pizza, but I could guzzle down a lemonade."

"Come on in."

***

The following day, Officers John Orion, Eddie Gierek and Matt Cantrell left the car park and were approached by three bearded black men in suits.

"Hello there, guys," one of them said.

"Hi there," Orion replied.

"What can we do for you?" Gierek asked.

"Are you from the West Indies?" Cantrell wanted to know.

"We're from a bank in Nassau in the Bahamas," one man told the cops. Then he startled, spotting something. "That car behind you! Quick, men, run!"

The three men sprinted toward their hired limousine, scrambled inside and sped away.

"Hey!" Gierek yelled.

The cops turned to look, but the car that had scared the bankers had driven away.

"That car terrified them!" Gierek shouted. "The bankers are scared they'll be targets!"

"We'll chase after the bankers," Cantrell said. "Get in the car!"

The three cops raced inside their civilian car. Gierek thrust his keys into the ignition, and in a matter of seconds, they were chasing the bankers' vehicle.

"The car behind was suspicious!" Gierek cried. "Calling all units, calling all units, a black limousine is driving toward Coral Gables. I repeat, Coral Gables!"

"You said Coral Gables?" Brogan replied over the radio.

"We got it!" Harmon told him. "Our squad van is on its way with Officers Brogan, Amy Cantrell, Post, Hayes and me!"

The contact ended, and Gierek accelerated toward the beach at Coral Gables. Then the bankers' car turned sharply and sped between two fences near the University of Miami. Another car violently rammed the limousine, and five bearded Cubans scrambled out of the vehicle, aimed their submachine guns and sprayed bullets through the windshield and side windows. All three bankers died instantly, riddled with bloody bullet wounds. Gierek's car arrived two seconds later, and the three cops hurried outside the vehicle, aiming their handguns and opening fire. Orion blazed toward two Cubans whilst Gierek blasted toward another two and Cantrell fired five rounds into the fifth brute. All five mobsters hurtled to the ground in rivers of blood.

But then, from the gaps between the bars of one of the fences, a man fired three shots into

Orion, then four shots into Gierek. Another guy pumped five bullets into Cantrell. All three cops fell hard onto the pavement, blood coming out of their mouths and spilling from their wounds. Both assassins then fled, and two cars drove past the three cops before the squad van swerved in to trap the cars.

Officers Brogan and Harmon, together with Amy, Helen and Patricia, leaped out, aimed their handguns and blasted toward more bearded Cubans who jumped out of both cars. Four shots from Amy felled two Cubans just as five blasts from Helen's firearm dropped another two and Patricia brought down the fifth thug. The women killed all five crooks in seconds, but the five criminals from the second car blazed toward the women with their submachine guns. The women dived toward the ground, and Brogan and Harmon used the distraction to their advantage. Brogan fired one round into a Cuban's head, another into a criminal's chest and two more rounds into a third brute's solar plexus. All three criminals hurtled backward. Harmon downed a fourth Cuban with one shot to the head, and the fifth with two blasts to the chest. Their wounds gushing blood, both thugs died instantly.

"Are there any more?" Harmon cried.

"There's no more!" Brogan replied.

"John, Eddie, Matt!" Amy screamed.

"Oh my God!" Patricia yelled.

"They're dead!" Helen cried.

The women sprinted toward the bloodied bodies of Orion, Gierek and Cantrell, and used their first aid skills to try to revive the three men. But their efforts were futile.

"Matt, Matt!" Amy sobbed. "Don't die on me, please!"

"I beg all three of you, don't die!" Patricia screamed. "No, no, no!"

Amy and Patricia fell into Brogan and Harmon's chests and sobbed uncontrollably. Helen was also whimpering violently.

***

Two hours later, all five officers were with Miles Erikson, Dave and Tony in the Miami PD changing room.

"Lieutenants Ross and Smith are on their way here," Erikson said. "They've just explained the situation to uniformed officers at the scene of the massacre. The three black men from the Bahamas were bankers. They had name badges and bank details on them. What they were doing here in Miami is anybody's guess."

"We must find out," Dave told him.

"By taking a flight to the Bahamas, then a boat trip to Nassau," Tony said.

"Before Ross and Smith arrive," Erikson said, "the five of you must explain what happened. Or do you want to leave it until later?"

The women were crying pitifully, tears soaking their feminine faces. Amy's hair was tied back, but two loose locks of hair draped down either side of her forehead, while Patricia's hair hung down to her shoulders with her forehead and face shining from the changing room's light. Helen's hair hung down over her face.

"We'll get it over with now," Patricia added. "I feel too sick to talk."

"Do you want to explain, Amy?" Helen said.

"I will," Amy replied. Choking on her emotions, she began. "Matt Cantrell was not only my husband; he was my best friend. No amount of training could've prepared me for his death and the violent deaths of John Orion and Eddie Gierek. Cantrell, Orion and Gierek were outstanding cops, the best of the best. Only Erikson, Brogan and Harmon were above their caliber. When the pathologist has examined my husband's body and we've solved the three murders, I must bury my husband. I don't think Cantrell, Orion and Gierek were killed by the arms dealers they were shooting at. I think they were killed by snipers firing from behind a fence, because of the angle the bullets entered their bodies. I don't know if the snipers were working for the arms dealers. The sooner we bury Cantrell and the other two, the better. My husband deserves a decent burial."

"We'll get Houston's forensics and CSI detectives to investigate the crime scene," Brogan promised Amy.

"Pretty soon," Harmon said, "Agents Bradley and Selma must take that trip to the Bahamas."

"Do the five of you want to take time off to receive trauma counseling?" Erikson wanted to know.

"No, Erikson," Helen pleaded. "We must carry on with the job."

"We mustn't let the team down," Patricia said.

"What I reckon we must do," Brogan said, "is visit Mount Sinai Hospital to see how Captain Siffrey is recovering. The five of us can support Siffrey as he helps us and comforts us through our loss."

"You have your heads screwed on straight," Dave remarked. "All you men and women."

Then Lieutenants Ken Ross and Alex Smith opened the changing room door and addressed the team.

"We heard about what happened, guys, ladies," Ross began.

"We're sorry about the deaths of Cantrell, Orion and Gierek," Smith said.

"They were good cops," Ross said. "And I mean outstanding. We've just come back from the scene of the shootout."

"We've also seen the photos and CCTV footage of the street outside Chief Mills's place," Smith informed Dave and Tony.

"Well done, Bradley, Selma," Ross said. "And well done you men and women for taking on those ten Cubans who killed our three guys."

"According to Amy," Dave told him, "it was snipers who murdered our three guys. Snipers working for the arms dealers. A total of fifteen arms dealers fired automatic weapons at our three guys, then at Brogan, Harmon and the three female cops who shot these arms dealers, eight cops against fifteen dealers. These Cubans also murdered three bankers from the Bahamas, after these men came over to Miami to report some news."

"The bankers' visit here is a mystery," Ross remarked.

Then Officer Dill came to the changing room door. "Agents Bradley and Selma?" he called.

"What is it?" Dave asked.

"Those four Americans and two Cubans who were at Mills's place," Dill said. "They're phoning us to pull a deal with you."

"I'll answer it," Dave told Dill.

Dave and Tony made their way to Captain Siffrey's office, Ross and Smith behind them, and Dave raised the receiver from the desk.

"You go ahead," Ross whispered.

"Hi, Agent Dave Bradley receiving your call," he said. "You're the four Americans and two Cubans who were with the two masked men who killed Chief Gary Mills. What do you want?"

"My name is Porlifio Diaz," a Cuban accent replied. "We only went to Chief Mills's place to intimidate him into leaving Calvera and Batista alone. But the two men in balaclavas got out of hand and murdered him. If you come over to Orlando, to the Flamingo Roadhouse, we'll tell you who the killers are, in exchange for immunity from prosecution. We want just you and Agent Selma there and no other cops. Otherwise, there will be a bloodbath. Just you and Selma. Meet us at the Flamingo Roadhouse outside Orlando in three hours' time. You got that?"

"We got it," Dave said.

The contact was cut off.

Dave lowered the receiver and told Ross and Smith what Diaz had said.

"The Flamingo Roadhouse south of Orlando," Ross said. "Porlifio Diaz is arranging a meet with you and Selma. You want us to send uniforms and Feds with you?"

"No, he said just us, and no other cops." Then Dave decided: "Selma, come with me."

"I got it," Selma replied.

***

Dave's car pulled in outside the Flamingo Roadhouse three hours later. Dave and Tony vacated the vehicle but saw signs of forced entry to the building. Pulling out their handguns, they entered the premises.

A shock awaited them. The two long-haired, bearded Cubans, including the guy with glasses, and the four bearded Americans were lying dead on the floor, their hands strapped behind their backs and their mouths gagged with silver duct tape. The sight filled the Feds with blind horror.

"Calvera and Batista's guys got to these guys before we did," Dave said.

"And it was a professional hit," Tony told him. "Tying the men up with straps, duct-taping their mouths and then shooting them each with two or three taps to the chest. Do you think the killers are still on the premises?"

"No, they're not," Dave said. "If they were, their vehicles would be outside."

"Freeze, Orlando Police!" a rough-voiced man yelled. "Drop your weapons and place your hands above your heads!"

Startled, Dave and Tony dropped their handguns and raised their hands together on top of their heads. Coming into the building were nine vice cops. The rough-voiced man had long blond hair, a mustache and was unshaven. A slim black man with short hair, a beard and glasses stood next to him. Then there was a Cuban man with long hair, a mustache and glasses, a black woman, a fair-haired woman and a Chinese American woman in front of two tall, solidly built black men with bald heads and glasses, and a handsome white guy with short dark hair. These armed men and women wore khaki trousers, and T-shirts.

"On the floor," the bearded black man growled.

"Are you the squad leader of Orlando Vice?" Dave asked.

"Yes, I am!" the black man snarled. "Get down on the floor!"

"And fast!" the mustached blond man growled.

"You're under arrest for the murders of Porlifio Diaz and his gang!" the black man announced.

"We're FBI!" Dave objected, as both men handcuffed him and Selma. "Look at our badges!"

"Arms dealers under Calvera and Batista murdered these six men, not us!" Tony told the men.

"Tell us that at Orlando PD," one of the tall black men told him.

***

In a jail cell at Orlando PD, Dave and Tony sat down on a bench. Six guards paced outside the row of cells. They included two slim black men with short beards and mustaches, a young black woman, a third bearded black guy and two bearded white men, one with short blond hair, the other with long brown hair. They were dressed in smart uniforms.

"When do we get out of here?" Tony demanded.

"When the captain is ready!" one of the black cops said.

"And not before!" another guy added.

Then the captain came into the corridor. He was a smartly dressed man with short brown hair and a mustache.

"Okay, officer," he addressed the black woman. "Open the cell door and release Agents Bradley and Selma."

"After what they did to those six arms dealers?" the woman asked.

"They're innocent," the captain told her. "The ballistics report could not match the bullets found in these men to the agents' handguns. The bullets were from AK-47 assault rifles. Release both agents."

The woman unlocked and opened the cell door. Dave and Tony came out and joined the captain, following him to his office.

"Thanks for releasing us," Tony said.

"Can we have our weapons back?" Dave enquired.

"And our ID?"

"Yes, you can," the captain replied. "But one question."

"Go on."

"If you're innocent, do you have any idea who could've massacred Porlifio Diaz and his mob?"

"Arms dealers working for Luis Calvera and Ramon Batista," Dave replied. "They wanted to silence the six men who were about to tell us who killed Chief Mills down in Miami. How Calvera and Batista knew Diaz and his mob were about to leak this information to us is anybody's guess."

"I'm sorry to hear about Mills's murder," the captain told him.

"He will not be missed," Dave remarked. "He was an evil, despicable man. Florida is a better place without him."

"Just one more question," Tony said.

"Go on."

"It's strange how a few minutes after Bradley and I entered the Flamingo Roadhouse and found Diaz's mob massacred, the nine men and women from Vice came in and arrested us," Tony said. "Somebody tipped them off we were coming, probably by phone. Who was it?"

"No doubt the men who murdered Porlifio Diaz and his mob," the captain said. "A Cuban guy phoned Orlando PD and tipped us off. I recognized his voice as being Luis Calvera's."

"Which brings me to one last question," Dave said. "Who tipped off Calvera that Diaz and his mob would meet us with the intention of telling us who Mills's killers were?"

"Your guess is as good as mine," the captain replied. "It's highly probable Calvera and Batista murdered Chief Mills in revenge for Mills intimidating them with a .45 Magnum, stealing their PIN numbers, bank details and forms, sending men to the Bahamas and having the arms dealers' three hundred million dollars wired through to Mills's bank in Orlando."

"Wait a minute!" Dave snapped. "How do you know all this information about the intimidation, the money laundering and the bank in Orlando?"

"Diaz phoned me and told me what Calvera and Batista had told him about what Chief Mills had done," the captain pointed out. "After Mills was murdered, the two killers went to the bank in Orlando, claimed to be Mills's brothers and confiscated the three hundred million dollars. Diaz told me each of the killers took a hundred million bucks, and the last hundred million was split six ways between Diaz and his five men."

"And then," Dave added. "Through interactions between Diaz's gang of six, the two killers and the Miami arms rings, Diaz's gang found out the three hundred million dollars had been stolen from Calvera and Batista, who would want them dead. Diaz phoned you and then us, but due to a tip-off, his gang was massacred."

"I suggest you both return to Miami and continue your investigation into Calvera and Batista's whereabouts," the captain said. "Good day."

"We'll do that," Tony agreed. "Good day."

"Let's move," Dave said.

***

Back at Miami PD, Lieutenants Ken Ross and Alex Smith greeted them.

"What's the news?" Ross asked.

"Only bad news," Dave replied. "When we entered the Flamingo Roadhouse outside Orlando, we found Porlifio Diaz and his five men bound, gagged with duct tape and shot to death. Then the Orlando vice squad arrested us, we spent a few hours detained at Orlando PD, and then the captain gave us back our weapons and ID and let us go."

"Mills's two killers had Diaz and his men silenced, so they could not betray the killers' identities," Tony added.

"More like it was Calvera and Batista's two mobs who murdered Diaz's gang, for either one of two motives," Dave suggested. "The killers had withdrawn the three hundred million dollars from the bank in Orlando, and each claimed one hundred million whilst the last one hundred million was split six ways between Diaz and his mob. Calvera and Batista wanted this money back, and both arms dealers sent their mobsters in with AK-47 assault rifles to attack Diaz's mob, tie them up and then kill them. Which means Calvera and Batista couldn't have been the two masked killers who murdered Mills, for Diaz and his mob wouldn't want to be close to two dangerous arms dealers who were pissed off about them claiming a hundred million bucks of their money. If the killers had been Calvera and Batista, they would've realized Diaz's plan sooner and murdered these six men long before they returned to Orlando. And Calvera and Batista would've withdrawn the three hundred million bucks from the bank in Orlando and claimed back all this money for themselves and their arms rings, without giving a hundred million to Diaz and his mob.

"The first possible motive is Calvera and Batista sent their guys in to massacre Diaz's mob in revenge for these mobsters claiming stolen money, which the arms dealers wanted back. The second motive is that Diaz was about to inform us who Chief Mills's killers were. Which means the killers were connected to Calvera and Batista's mobs, and the arms dealers wanted Diaz and his men silenced. And it was Calvera who phoned Orlando PD after the massacre to inform the captain that Diaz and his men were dead and blamed us two Feds for the murders. Which is why the Orlando vice squad arrested us when we arrived, before we were cleared due to forensic evidence and the ballistics report. Because Calvera made the call, it was Calvera's men who massacred Diaz's guys.

"But how did Calvera and Batista know Diaz was about to tell us who Mills's killers were? Only two groups of people knew Diaz was going to rat on Calvera's mob and the two killers under his payroll. Diaz and his mob, who made the call, and all the cops here at Miami PD who received the call. One or more cops in this department must've phoned Calvera and tipped him off that Agent Selma and I were about to drop in on Diaz's men."

"That's impossible," Tony said. "Nobody in this department has Calvera's telephone number or cell number or email address. More likely, Calvera and Batista's guys murdered Diaz and his men to reclaim one hundred million dollars and are after the two killers. Which means Mills's killers are not working for the arms rings. They are probably dirty cops or people from internal affairs who double-crossed and murdered Mills before withdrawing the other two hundred million bucks from Mills's account in Orlando. If the killers are working for the arms rings, they would've returned the two hundred million to the arms dealers on top of the one hundred million taken from Diaz's mob.

"But when Calvera phoned the captain at Orlando PD to tell him we'd massacred Diaz's guys at the Flamingo Roadhouse, how could Calvera have possibly known we would be there when only Diaz's men and the guys at Miami PD knew about this meeting? I think you're right, Dave. A dirty cop here at Miami PD called or emailed Calvera to warn him us Feds would meet up with Diaz, who would tell us who Mills's assassins were."

"Everything will make more sense later," Dave told Tony. "Right now, we must take a flight to the Bahamas, then a boat trip to Nassau to visit that offshore bank. We'll find out which people from internal affairs wired the arms dealers three hundred million dollars through to that bank in Orlando, and also what those three black men in suits were doing here in Miami. The three bankers wanted to tell us some critical information before they saw a mobster's vehicle in the street behind Orion, Gierek and Cantrell, drove away terrified and were then massacred by those fifteen mobsters at Coral Gables."

"We'll get the FBI to fly you to the Bahamas in an hour's time," Smith said.

"I'll call Chief Robert Hook at Miami's FBI headquarters now," Ross promised both agents. "The plane will fly you straight to Nassau, then refuel while you visit the bank. When you've done your job, the plane will fly you back to Miami."

"We appreciate that, Lieutenants Ross and Smith," Tony thanked them.

"We'll drive to the FBI headquarters now," Dave told Tony.

***

The FBI plane sped through the sky from Florida to Nassau. Flying the plane was a female pilot. With Dave and Tony were

Chief Hook and Agents Brown and Bragan. The plane touched down on an airstrip and came to a halt. Hook opened the side door, and Dave and Tony emerged.

"Nassau is over there, to the left," Hook said.

"Thank you," Dave replied.

"Let's go," Tony said.

They reached Nassau in ten minutes and approached the bank.

But getting out of a squad van were four vice cops dressed in khaki trousers, formal shirts and leather jackets. The first was a black guy with a mustache and glasses. The second man was also black with short hair turning gray and a small beard and mustache around his chin and mouth, but no sideburns. The third guy was mixed race with long hair, sharp eyes and a medium-length beard and mustache. The fourth man was white with long dark hair, a beard and glasses. These men approached Dave and Tony.

"Excuse me, are you FBI Agents Dave Bradley and Tony Selma?" the gray-haired bearded man asked. "I'm Squad Leader Bill Faraday, who commands the American vice squad sent over here from Florida."

"I'm Officer Benton," the mustached black man said.

"Officer Sheridan," the long-haired, bearded guy told Dave.

"And I'm Officer Deplin," the white guy with glasses added.

"We can't allow you to enter the bank," Bill Faraday said.

"First of all," Dave retorted, "how do you know we're FBI Agents Dave Bradley and Tony Selma? Secondly, who sent you over to this island to intercept us? And thirdly, why aren't we allowed inside the bank?"

"Do you know that's obstructing a federal investigation?" Tony pointed out.

"Those are our orders," Benton said.

"Orders from who?" Dave asked.

"From Captain Denzel Forizo," Deplin replied.

"And he's not a man you want to cross," Sheridan warned the two Feds. "He was discharged from his job in Miami for corruption and brutality."

"Along with all of us," Benton added.

"Well, tell Captain Denzel Forizo I don't scare easily," Dave said.

"Even more to the point," Tony said. "Who sent you guys to obstruct our investigation?"

"Are you connected to two arms dealers, Luis Calvera and Ramon Batista?" Dave wanted to know.

"You'd be forgiven for thinking that," Faraday said. "But no, there's no connection."

"You were discharged for corruption and brutality," Tony pointed out.

"We were desperate to convict two pimps who were beating up call girls," Faraday told him. "So we roughed up these pimps, planted flick-knives on them to make it look like self-defense and stole their money to fund better lives for the hookers these men controlled. Chief Gary Mills found out, had us dispatched and sent us over here to investigate drug dealing and money laundering in the Bahamas."

"We wanted to kill him," Sheridan said.

"And we made plans," Benton boasted.

"Did you kill him?" Dave asked.

"No, Bradley," Faraday replied.

"Somebody else got to him first," Deplin muttered.

"Are you working with Chief Mills's killers to get us off the case?" Dave asked.

"We don't even know who Mills's killers were," Sheridan replied.

"But Captain Forizo received a message on his telephone from a guy with a distorted voice," Faraday told the Feds. "This guy told Forizo you Feds were coming over to this island to ask questions that would connect the

Florida arms dealers to Mills's murder. He was probably an arms dealer who promised us a shipload of weapons to combat drug dealers and pimps over here, but it could've been a guy from internal affairs or Miami PD. We hate arms dealers, but we disobey internal affairs and we'll be on the streets claiming social security."

"We can keep this investigation secret between us," Dave said. "Let us inside the bank, and we'll find out who, on behalf of internal affairs, wired dirty money from the arms dealers' offshore account over to Florida. Then we'll mount another investigation into who called Forizo."

"Now you're testing the water," Benton muttered.

"You're really taking liberties, you guys," Sheridan warned the Feds.

"We have no guarantee your investigation won't land us and Captain Forizo on the streets of Miami, wondering where our careers went," Deplin told them.

"But hear this," Faraday said. "People who interfere with dirty cops or arms dealers end up at the bottom of the ocean with their chests full of lead."

"Are you threatening us?" Dave asked.

"We're telling you," Sheridan retorted.

"It's a warning," Benton replied.

"But we'll only pull the trigger on criminals who pull the trigger on you," Faraday promised the Feds. "Not the other way round. Okay, guys, we'd better let these guys from the FBI enter the bank and mount their investigation into the dirty money."

The vice cops climbed into their squad van and drove away.

"Not the nicest I've met," Tony told Dave.

"I've met worse," Dave remarked. "Let's make our way inside."

***

Inside the bank, Dave requested to see the manager. The black woman, who had served Lieutenants Ross and Smith a few days before, approached the Feds.

"Hi, I'm the manager," she announced. "My name's Judith Grander. How can I help you?"

"FBI Agents Dave Bradley and Tony Selma," Dave said. "My first question. Did you send three bankers in blue suits over to Miami to report to us criminal activities involving arms money? Three black men with beards?"

"Yes, I did," Judith said. "Are they alright?"

"No, they're not," Dave said. "They were shot to death in an alleyway between Coral Gables and the University of Miami by men working for arms dealers Luis Calvera and Ramon Batista. Three vice cops were killed in the same attack by two snipers, probably the same men who murdered Chief Mills, but we cannot identify them."

"Our three bankers were killed!" Judith exclaimed.

"I'm afraid so."

"We're both sorry," Tony said.

"Before they died," Dave said, "the bankers spotted a mobsters' vehicle positioned behind the three vice cops who were massacred by the snipers. We don't know whether the snipers or the men who murdered Chief Mills were arms dealers or dirty cops or people from internal affairs."

"You keep saying Chief Mills was murdered?" Judith asked. "And this means he was a cop who sent two men in suits to launder Calvera and Batista's arms money into his bank account in Orlando, Florida. The two men who visited this bank a few days ago told me Mills ran a law firm in this city, and Calvera and Batista had joined his firm. The two men visiting were lawyers. But now you're telling me Calvera and Batista are arms dealers who had our bankers killed at Coral Gables, Mills embezzled their money using these two guys from internal affairs, and then Mills was murdered. There was no law firm in Orlando. But our three bankers must've spotted incriminating information on our computers; that's why they flew over to Miami. And that's why they died."

"We believe so," Tony said.

"You mind if we check this info?" Dave asked.

"Go ahead," Judith replied. "They actually downloaded photos from a computer screen showing cash withdrawals in Orlando."

"We must see this," Tony said.

"Come with me," Judith said.

All three of them walked into the bank's back room, where Judith displayed the CCTV photos sent from the bank in Orlando. And in these photos were three checks being held by two men, each check being a hundred million dollars. Both men were bearded, one with long black hair, the other with short gray hair. Behind these men were Porlifio Diaz and his five mobsters.

"Those two guys!" Dave said. "They're dirty cops, but they're not from internal affairs! They're Lieutenants Ken Ross and Alex Smith!"

"Oh my God!" Tony exclaimed.

"The same two guys who visited this bank a few days ago and wired the arms dealers' money through to Mills's bank account in Orlando," Judith said. "Under the false pretense that Mills, Calvera and Batista and these two guys worked for a law firm in Orlando, a law firm that never existed.

"The enormous amount of money involved made the bank staff suspicious, so they took these images from CCTV footage captured inside the bank, then sent these photos over to us. The manager of the bank in Orlando contacted me and my three bankers, whom I then sent to Miami to report the skullduggery this manager told us about."

"That gang of six men behind Ken Ross and Alex Smith are Porlifio Diaz and his mob," Tony pointed out.

"Not only that," Dave added, "Ken Ross and Alex Smith probably killed Chief Mills, then claimed two hundred million bucks with two of the checks, whilst the third check was given to Diaz and his mob. When Diaz phoned Miami PD from the Flamingo Roadhouse, only Ross and Smith were in the captain's office to overhear Diaz contacting me. After we set off on our three-hour journey to this roadhouse, Ross and Smith made a call to Luis Calvera somewhere in Florida, and Calvera and Batista sent their guys to massacre Diaz and his men. By the time Tony and I entered the roadhouse, all of them were shot to death and, due to Calvera phoning Orlando PD, the Orlando vice squad arrested us for the massacre. Ross and Smith tipped off Calvera and Batista that Diaz and his mob would rat about who killed Chief Mills."

"But we have no concrete evidence to pin Mills's murder on Ross and Smith," Tony said.

"This is only supposition," Judith said.

"You're right," Tony replied.

"But there's something else," Dave said. "Those four vice cops who tried to stop us entering this bank. Captain Denzel Forizo received a call about us coming over from Miami to Nassau to investigate the money laundering. Nobody at Miami PD knew we would drop in on Diaz and his mob, and nobody there knew we would take this FBI flight here. Except Lieutenants Ross and Smith. Lieutenants Ross and Smith made that call to Captain Forizo, Ross distorting his voice and promising Forizo and his Miami vice cops that if they stopped us entering the bank, they'd be paid dirty money from arms dealers to fund their war against drug dealers and pimps here in the Bahamas. Ross and Smith ordered these guys to stop us entering the bank to cover up their visit a few days ago where they laundered the arms dealers' three hundred million bucks into Mills's bank account in Florida."

Tony turned toward Judith. "You have CCTV cameras watching all corners of this bank?"

"Yes, we do."

"You mind if we look at CCTV from a few days ago, then take the footage along with this lot of photos incriminating Ross and Smith?"

"I'll show you the CCTV footage."

In the footage, they saw the two lieutenants talking to Judith before transferring the three hundred million dollars from the Bahamas to Mills's bank in Florida.

"Lieutenants Ross and Smith again," Dave observed.

"The two masked men who murdered Mills," Tony said. "They were big, tall and strongly built. Just like Lieutenants Ross and Smith. CCTV footage picked up the masked men with Diaz's mobsters at Little Havana, and then Ross and Smith with Diaz's guys withdrawing those three checks from that bank in Orlando."

"We have to prove Ross and Smith made those two phone calls to Calvera and then Captain Forizo," Dave told Tony. "Which requires another visit to the call center so we can get the records from those calls."

"But it will be hard to prove Ross and Smith murdered Chief Mills," Tony said. "They could pin the murder on Calvera and Batista, using the defense that these arms dealers were behind the massacre of Diaz and his mob."

"One thing at a time," Dave insisted. He turned to Judith. "Can we have photos of Ross and Smith wiring this money through to Florida?"

"I'll print them out now."

She worked her printer, and the machine gave five photos of Ross and Smith meeting with her and transferring the money to Florida.

"Thanks," Dave said, then addressed Tony. "We'll fold all these photos, place them in a small envelope and I'll hide the envelope in the inner pocket of my leather jacket, zipped up."

Dave did what he'd said, then both Feds shook hands with Judith.

"It's been nice doing business with you," Tony told her. "We'd better leave. Good day."

"Good day," Dave repeated. "Have a nice day."

***

Dave and Tony left the bank and walked through Nassau to the airstrip. But four men grabbed the Feds, threw them against the squad van, restrained and handcuffed them.

"Hey!" Dave cried. "What's going on?"

"Shut up!" Faraday growled.

"Forizo wants to see you," Benton said.

"Don't give us any trouble!" Sheridan roared.

"Along with handcuffing these Feds, do we gag them?" Deplin asked.

"Thrust the gags in their mouths," Faraday ordered, "so they can't call for help."

Benton and Sheridan pulled two white gags out of their leather jacket pockets, forced them into Dave and Tony's mouths and tied them behind their heads. Dave and Tony cried muffled groans through the gags and were manhandled inside the van and forced to lie face-down on the floor. Benton, Sheridan and Deplin aimed their handguns toward Dave and Tony whilst Squad Leader Faraday banged his keys into the ignition.

The van sped out of Nassau. Dave and Tony were petrified with terror, fearing that Captain Denzel Forizo would have them executed with gunshots to their heads.

The van stopped outside Captain Forizo's property overlooking a garden. The vehicle's side door was slid open, and Benton, Sheridan and Deplin manhandled Dave and Tony outside into the garden. Faraday emerged through the driver's door, and Captain Forizo greeted them. He was a tall, muscular black man with a medium-length beard and wearing sunglasses.

"Hi there," Forizo began. "Remove the gags and handcuffs."

Benton and Sheridan untied the gags, pulled them out of the agents' mouths and then unlocked the handcuffs. Dave and Tony wiped the sweat from their faces and then rubbed their wrists.

"So, you're Captain Forizo?" Dave asked.

"We heard how you and your four guys from Miami roughed up two pimps, had them detained, stole their money and funded better lives for the hookers you freed from these men," Tony said.

"So much for being real good Samaritans!" Dave shouted. "Chief Mills found out, and had you sent to the Bahamas."

"Now Mills is dead," Tony said, "you're welcome to return to Florida and help us nail the two lieutenants who murdered him. Namely Ken Ross and Alex Smith."

"And spare our lives," Dave said.

"We'll spare your lives anyway," Forizo said. "But we're happy to catch the sun here whilst we combat drug dealers and pimps who terrorize these islands, once the guy who phoned me, ordering me to stop you entering the bank, delivers that next shipment of weapons or money he promised us."

"There'll be no weapons or money," Dave told him. "For it wasn't arms dealers or men from internal affairs who made that call. Ross and Smith made that call, but Ross made an empty promise. Even if you guys had stopped us entering the bank, Ross and Smith were never about to deliver arms or money. They're dirty cops and they're too greedy. These guys laundered the arms dealers' money into Mills's bank account in Florida, and when they killed Mills, they impersonated Mills's brothers and withdrew all this money for themselves and Diaz's guys. When Diaz's guys were murdered by Calvera and Batista's guys, the arms dealers stole back a hundred million of the three hundred million bucks Ross and Smith stole from them. But Ross and Smith still have two hundred million and have no intention of sharing even one dollar with you vice cops."

"Wait a minute," Forizo snapped. "How do you know Ross and Smith murdered Mills? And how do you know Ross made that phone call to me?"

"We don't," Dave replied. "It's only supposition. But only Ross and Smith knew we were taking the FBI plane to Nassau a few hours ago, and only they would have a motive for preventing us entering the bank. We have circumstantial evidence, but now we need forensic and DNA evidence. If you return with us to Miami and help us bring down Ross and Smith, you'll gain a handsome sum of money to fund your war against drug dealers and pimps."

"I like your attitude," Forizo said. "But I'm afraid we must turn down your offer. It is too easy for criminals to get lost in the underworld of Miami whilst it's not so easy for them to get lost here in the Bahamas, each island having a smaller population. That's why it's easier for us to track down criminals on these islands than in the concrete jungle of Miami and the rest of Florida."

"Have it your way," Dave said.

"But out of gratitude," Forizo remarked, "my men will drive both you Feds to the airstrip near the beach outside Nassau. Save you walking."

"We appreciate that," Dave replied.

"Thank you," Tony said.

***

With Faraday driving the squad van, Benton, Sheridan and Deplin were sat in the van's main compartment, Dave and Tony positioned behind them.

"You saved us both a long walk to the airstrip," Dave told the vice cops.

"But your offer was cool," Benton praised Dave.

"We felt tempted to take you up on it," Sheridan added.

"But we're needed here in the Bahamas to stop arms dealers, drug dealers and pimps spreading terror and misery through these islands," Deplin remarked. "We don't like scum like them ruining these islands and intimidating people."

"When we're ready," Faraday said, "we'll return to Miami and continue the fight against vice and drug dealing, but we must clean up these islands first. And now, we're at the airstrip."

"Thanks, guys," Dave said. "We'll look forward to seeing you again."

"Chief Hook and Agents Brown and Bragan are waiting outside the FBI plane," Tony reminded Dave. "We'd better go. Good day, guys."

Dave and Tony vacated the vehicle and ran toward Hook, Brown and Bragan.

"We've refueled the plane," Hook told them.

"But what happened to you guys?" Bragan wanted to know.

"Were you kidnapped by vice cops?" Brown asked.

"We were," Tony replied.

"But then they let us go," Dave said.

"Get on the plane," Brown ordered. "We're about to go."

All five Feds made their way through the side door and into the FBI plane before Hook slammed shut the door.

***

At Mount Sinai Hospital, Amy, Helen and Patricia sat beside Captain Siffrey's bed. Siffrey was still in a coma. Their dark hair tied back in ponytails, Amy and Patricia pulled out two tubes of dark red lipstick and painted their lips, before putting the lipsticks away and wiping the sweat off their foreheads and feminine faces. Helen's brown hair hung down to her shoulders. The hospital atmosphere was so calm and quiet one could hear a pin drop.

Then Amy's cell phone bleeped, and she answered.

"Amy Cantrell here. Who is it?"

A Cuban man answered with a very strong Floridian accent. "A briefcase has been left in the ladies' toilet on the hospital's ground floor. We believe it's an explosive device. We need you women cops to come quickly to give us a second opinion. Shall we evacuate the ground floor?"

"Not yet," Amy told him. "We're coming down."

She hung up.

"What is it?" Patricia asked.

"A bomb scare," Amy told the other two. "A briefcase that may be an explosive device has been left in the ground floor's ladies' toilet. But it may be a hoax."

"We'd better check it out," Helen advised them.

"And fast!" Patricia cried.

The three women took the elevator down to the ground floor and ran the short distance to the ladies' room. They saw doctors, nurses and hospital security clearing the area.

"The briefcase is beside one of the toilet cubicles," the head of security told the women.

"Call the bomb squad," Helen ordered.

"We'll check it out," Patricia said.

The women pushed the door open and entered the ladies' room. And they found the briefcase but heard no timer ticking.

"It's harmless," Helen told her two partners. "There's no explosive device."

Then three bearded Cubans stormed out of the cubicles and pointed their rifles at the women's heads.

"What's the meaning of this?" Helen cried.

"Shut up, lady!" one Cuban whispered, his voice savage. "We have our rifles trained on you! Put your hands together behind your backs! And don't scream or fight us! You're coming with us! You guys, get the straps to tie the women's arms behind their backs. I've also cut three strips of tape to gag them with. Hurry up!"

Amy, Patricia and Helen joined their hands behind their backs, and two Cubans tied their wrists with black straps. With the women securely tied up, the Cubans spun the women round to face them.

"You won't get away with this," Amy said.

"Kidnapping and murdering three cops is a capital crime," Patricia said.

Amy, Helen and Patricia gave muffled cries as the white tape was pressed over their mouths and tight against their cheeks. They struggled to breathe through the gags.

"We'll use you young ladies as hostages," one Cuban snapped. "Calvera and Batista want to see you."

With their rifles against the women's heads and their muscular arms restraining them, the Cubans pushed the women out of the ladies' room, through reception to the entrance. The staff panicked at seeing the women tied up with their mouths taped.

"Don't try anything stupid," one Cuban said. "Or we'll blow the women's heads off."

"There is no bomb," a second Cuban said. "It's a hoax. Let us pass and nobody will get hurt."

The security guards, doctors and nurses backed up away from the Cubans, and the Cubans pushed Amy, Helen and Patricia through the entrance door and outside the building. Coming out of a getaway van's front seats were two more bearded Cubans, who opened the van's back doors. Whilst making terrified groans, Amy, Helen and Patricia were manhandled into the vehicle's main compartment before their three bearded attackers climbed in and the other two men climbed back into the front seats. After shutting all doors, the driver started the ignition, and the van sped away.

***

Officers Erikson, Brogan, Harmon and Dill arrived at the hospital ten minutes later.

"What happened?" Erikson asked the head of security.

"Three Cubans made a bomb threat hoax," the man said. "They told us, and we cleared the area around the ladies' room, where they'd left a briefcase. One of them called the three female cops, who came down in the elevator. When the women entered the ladies' room to investigate, the Cubans threatened them and tied them up. They came out with the cops as hostages and told us the bomb scare was a hoax. They pushed the women toward a getaway van, met two other Cubans and pushed the women into the van. Then, all five Cubans drove away with the kidnapped women. The men were tall or of medium height, strongly built with short hair and beards."

"Thanks," Nathan Dill said. "We have a kidnapping on our hands."

"And you know who's behind it," Harmon remarked.

"Luis Calvera and Ramon Batista," Brogan replied.

"Has the briefcase been checked and removed?" Dill added.

"It has," the security man told the young black cop.

"First, we'll check on Captain Siffrey," Erikson said. "I'll call Lieutenants Ross and Smith to report the kidnapping and get squad cars in the area to hunt for a getaway van. What color was the van?"

"It was blue," the security man replied.

"We're on it," Brogan said.

"You three, check on Captain Siffrey," Erikson ordered. "I'll check CCTV footage of the blue getaway van and its license plate, call units all over Miami and then report the kidnapping to Ross and Smith."

***

As soon as the FBI plane landed outside Miami's FBI headquarters, Dave and Tony disembarked, flanked by the female pilot and with Agents Hook, Brown and Bragan. Dave and Tony climbed into the civilian car and sped toward Miami PD before coming to a stop, getting out and running toward the forensics lab. They met Pathologist Lee Houston and CSI Officers Tom Cornelli, Robert Watts and Rick Jackson.

"Any news on the ballistics report and where the shots came from that killed Orion, Gierek and Cantrell?" Dave asked. "Amy Cantrell told me snipers killed the three men because the gunshots hit the men from an angle. Meaning the shots came from one of the fences enclosing the street outside Coral Gables."

"Amy was right," Houston said. "And the shots that killed these three cops came from two automatic revolvers. The same weapons that killed Chief Mills, and the two snipers were probably the same men behind Mills's death. But the revolvers are missing, so we can't trace the weapons to the owners or the arms dealers who supplied them to the two killers. We found fibers from woolen gloves on the rounds, which means the same guys who popped Mills also murdered Officers Orion, Gierek and Cantrell.

"Also—about the fifteen Cubans who shot to death those three bankers—"

"What about them?" Tony asked.

"The serial numbers on their rifles and submachine guns enabled us to trace the weapons back to Luis Calvera and Ramon Batista," Houston said. "We don't want a war with Cuba. Calvera and Batista used to have diplomatic immunity, but not anymore."

"How do we nail both arms dealers without enraging the Cuban government?" Tony asked Dave.

"We tell the Cuban government of crimes and murders Calvera and Batista committed in Cuba," Dave replied. "Other than that, it's down to Florida's state government and the boys in the White House to negotiate an agreement with the Cubans by which Calvera and Batista and their mobs are sent straight to death row."

"But there's bad news," Jackson informed the Feds.

"Who will tell Bradley and Selma?" Watts asked him quietly.

"Houston should tell them," Cornelli said.

"You say there's bad news?" Dave asked.

"Yeah, there is," Houston told him. "Amy Cantrell, Helen Post and Patricia Hayes have been kidnapped. They were abducted from Mount Sinai Hospital before you arrived back from the Bahamas. Calvera and Batista have got them."

"Oh my God!" Dave exclaimed.

"We must check the mobsters' van and its license plate from CCTV footage and then put an APB out on the vehicle," Tony growled. "Find out where the getaway van is heading.

"And in any case, we have other reasons to check the CCTV footage in the computer room. Before those three bankers were killed outside Coral Gables, they saw a mobsters' vehicle and ran for their lives, terrified. The mobsters in the vehicle made a call to the fifteen Cubans at Coral Gables, and the Cubans cornered the bankers and shot them to death. The mobsters in the vehicle may have been the two snipers who killed Orion, Gierek and Cantrell."

"We don't know it was mobsters in the vehicle who called the bankers' killers," Dave replied. "At that bank in the Bahamas, Judith Grander had incriminating CCTV footage from both the bank in the Bahamas and the one in Florida which shows two high-ranking cops whom we can't name laundering mob money into Mills's account in Florida, then withdrawing this money in three checks after Mills died. Judith sent the three bankers to Miami to inform Orion, Gierek and Cantrell. The two dirty cops inside the vehicle the bankers saw must have realized the bankers knew too much, and that's why the bankers died. The three vice cops would have hatched on that these dirty cops were behind the corruption and the bankers' murders, so the dirty cops were the snipers who killed the men from Vice.

"We must make four trips, the first trip to the computer room. The second will be another visit to the crime scene outside Coral Gables to detect any new forensic evidence.

The third will be back here to submit this evidence over to you CSI officers. And the fourth will be to the call center to check the records for incriminating phone calls between the two dirty cops and the arms dealers. Let's get onto it, Tony."

"I'm with you," Tony said.

***

In the computer room, Dave and Tony ordered a woman to check the CCTV footage from outside Miami PD to the street behind the main street where the bankers had met up with Orion, Gierek and Cantrell.

"The bankers encounter Orion, Gierek and Cantrell in the main street outside Miami PD," Dave said as he watched the footage. "A car pulling up down the street behind the three vice cops spooks the bankers and they scramble into their hired car. Can you zoom in on the car behind? It belongs to Lieutenants Ross and Smith. It's a squad car. There are two bearded men in the front seats, one with long black hair, the other with short gray hair. That's Ross and Smith."

"Are you saying Lieutenants Ross and Smith are dirty?" the woman asked, her voice frantic.

"It's becoming more likely," Tony told her.

"But keep it to yourself until we arrest them," Dave ordered. "And that goes for everybody here. Now we'll check the enlarged photo from the CCTV cameras at the hospital, showing the blue van driven by the five bearded Cubans. We'll check the license plate."

The woman downloaded the CCTV footage taken of the getaway van outside the Mount Sinai Hospital and gave them the license plate.

"Do an APB on the van, and we'll detect where it's heading," Dave told her. "Tony, we're heading for that alleyway between Coral Gables and the University of Miami."

***

At the alleyway outside Coral Gables, Dave and Tony passed through a gate toward the fence of metal bars from which the two snipers had shot and killed Officers Orion, Gierek and Cantrell.

"The snipers wore gloves," Tony said. "That's why no DNA was found behind this fence."

"They were not wearing sneakers like they did when they murdered Chief Mills," Dave told Tony. "They were wearing normal shoes, by the shoeprints in the mud. The patterns on those shoeprints are the same patterns as on the shoes worn by Lieutenants Ross and Smith. But they were also not wearing balaclavas to hide their identities. I see hairs on the metal bars, black hairs and gray hairs. Those are hairs from their beards. We'll collect them in the evidence bags."

"There's something else," Tony observed. "The shoeprints lead through the mud toward dry mud, which has been disturbed. This disturbed mud is surrounded by solid mud."

They traced the shoeprints to the disturbed soil, and then dug it up. They found the woolen gloves and the two automatic revolvers.

"These were the two pairs of woolen gloves and the two automatic revolvers used to murder Mills, and then our three men from Vice," Dave said. "Ross and Smith's DNA will be inside the gloves. We must run these over to the forensics lab."

"But because Ross and Smith have never been convicted of criminal offenses," Tony said, "their DNA profiles won't turn up on the DNA database."

"I'll find a way of collecting their DNA without them knowing," Dave promised him.

***

At the Forensics Lab, Dave and Tony handed Lee Houston the evidence bags containing the black and gray hairs, the two automatic revolvers and two pairs of gloves.

"These hairs are from the snipers' beards," Dave informed him. "You can extract DNA samples from these hairs and from inside the gloves, DNA and sweat. DNA will also have collected onto the revolvers used to kill Chief Mills, and later Officers John Orion, Eddie Gierek and Matt Cantrell."

"We know Lieutenants Ross and Smith murdered Mills, and later Officers Orion, Gierek and Cantrell," Tony said. "But even though their DNA profiles are not on the DNA database, you can use the revolvers' serial numbers to trace the revolvers back to their owners, namely Ross and Smith."

"Are you serious?" Houston asked. "Ross and Smith are highly respected police officers with super clean records. What possible motive could they have for killing Mills?"

"Mills hired them to launder arms money from the arms dealers' offshore account in the Bahamas into his account in Florida," Tony said. "They were greedy for this money, so they murdered Mills, then drove with Porlifio Diaz's mob to the bank in Orlando and, whilst posing as Mills's brothers, they withdrew all the money, kept two hundred million dollars for themselves and paid a hundred million to Diaz's mob. We also know Ross and Smith phoned Calvera and Batista, telling them Diaz was about to pin Mills's murder on them and Diaz's mob had a hundred million bucks of Calvera's money. Other than Diaz's mob, only the cops at Miami PD knew Diaz was about to rat on the two killers, and only Ross and Smith were in the office to overhear Diaz's phone call. Only they could've phoned Calvera and Batista. But we have to prove it. Which requires one more trip to the call center. Whilst you match the bullets to the two revolvers, collect DNA and trace the revolvers back to Ross and Smith, Agent Bradley and I will be off to the call center to get recordings of those calls."

"Let's go," Dave said.

***

At the call center, Dave and Tony ordered the middle-aged blonde woman and the young dark-haired man to scan all Ross's phone calls and cell phone calls from the last few days. The first cell phone call was from the street outside Miami PD, telling the fifteen Cubans how the three bankers from Nassau were about to expose money laundering carried out by Ross and Smith, and both cops wanted the bankers dead to cover up this crime. They ordered the Cubans to pursue the bankers' hired car and kill the bankers.

The second call was to Calvera's new hideout, informing Calvera and Batista of how Diaz had a hundred million bucks of Calvera's money and was about to meet up with Dave and Tony to pin Mills's murder on Calvera and Batista. The third call was to Captain Denzel Forizo in the Bahamas, ordering Forizo and his four vice cops to prevent Dave and Tony entering the bank in Nassau. The fourth call was again to Calvera's hideout, telling Calvera Amy, Helen and Patricia were at the hospital, and he must send a gang of Cubans to set up a bomb hoax and have the women kidnapped.

"Ross made those four calls," Dave said. "We have them recorded on tape as evidence.

Now can you pinpoint the exact location of Calvera's calls to Ross, and we'll find Calvera's hideout?"

"And through finding Calvera's hideout," Tony said, "we'll find Amy, Helen and Patricia."

"I'm on it," the dark-haired man said.

After ten minutes, he had traced Calvera's reply call.

"It's number twenty-three Palm Lane, just north of Miami."

"Twenty-three Palm Lane," Dave repeated. "I'll write that down. We got it."

"What's our next move?" Tony said.

"We stop off at a liquor store to buy a couple of lemonades," Dave told the young man. "I'm thirsty. Are you?"

"You bet." Tony chuckled.

***

While Tony waited outside Miami PD's main office, Dave entered and approached Lieutenants Ken Ross and Alex Smith, carrying one of the two bottles of lemonade he had bought for himself and Tony.

"Hi there," Dave said.

"Hi, Bradley," Ross and Smith both said. "How did the bank trip in the Bahamas go?"

"We had no luck," Dave lied. "Four vice cops from Florida barred us from going inside, kidnapped us and dumped us in the clutches of Captain Denzel Forizo. But Forizo released us, and we returned to Miami."

"We're sorry to hear that," Ross said.

"But one favor," Dave added. "It's hot, and I must remove my leather jacket. You mind holding my lemonade?"

"Sure, Bradley," Ross replied.

Dave passed the bottle to Ross, and Ross held the plastic container tightly. Dave slipped off his jacket and hung it on a chair. Then he retrieved the lemonade.

"I appreciate that," Dave told Ross. "Thanks. Have a nice day."

"Have a nice day," Ross replied.

Dave vacated the main office.

***

With empty bottles of lemonade in their hands, Dave and Tony entered the forensics lab.

"We matched the bullets to the two revolvers and traced ownership of these weapons back to Lieutenants Ross and Smith," Houston said. "But their DNA profiles are not on the DNA database."

"I have Ross's DNA," Dave replied. "On my lemonade bottle. See if there's a match."

"You're smart, Bradley," Houston said.

"Bradley always gets results," Tony told him.

It was the work of four or five minutes to match Ross's DNA on the lemonade bottle to the DNA samples collected from inside one pair of woolen gloves and one of the revolvers.

"We have a match!" Houston enthused.

"Sadly, we couldn't get Smith's DNA samples," Tony informed Houston and his three CSI detectives.

"But we'll still link Smith to the murders in Little Havana and Coral Gables as we did Ross," Dave told him. "We found out through tracing Calvera's reply calls to Ross that Calvera's hideout is twenty-three Palm Lane on Miami's outskirts.

"Against Calvera and Batista's mobs, we only have Tony and myself, backed up by Squad Leader Erikson and Officers Brogan, Harmon and Dill. That's six of us attempting to rescue Amy, Helen and Patricia, and we'll be heavily outnumbered. We need backup from you, Houston and Detectives Jackson, Watts and Cornelli. A total of ten cops armed with rifles."

"Why not get backup from the Feds and the uniforms?" Houston asked.

"They're not always discreet," Dave replied. "We lose the element of surprise, and Amy, Helen and Patricia are dead. We must drive over to Palm Lane in a squad van and two civilian cars, but we need assistance from you, forensics and CSI officers. You can also collect forensic evidence when the rescue is over. Your assistance is a must."

"Okay, Bradley," Houston agreed. He turned to Officers Jackson, Watts and Cornelli. "We're needed at twenty-three Palm Lane."

Dave used his cell phone to contact Erikson, Brogan, Harmon and Dill at Mount Sinai Hospital.

"Hi, Erikson," he said. "We need you to join us at twenty-three Palm Lane. That's where Calvera is holding captive the women cops."

"We'll head there now," Erikson replied.

The contact ended, and Dave, Tony and the four CSI detectives made their way to the weapons room to collect six high-caliber rifles.

***

Lieutenants Ross and Smith were already in Ross's squad car, for they had hatched on to Dave's plan.

"Agents Bradley and Selma are onto us," Ross snapped.

"Bradley gave you that lemonade bottle to get your DNA, so he could match it to the DNA samples found on your revolver and inside your gloves," Smith snarled.

"Not only that," Ross growled, "his body language told me he was lying about not being able to enter the bank in the Bahamas. Through CCTV footage from the banks in Orlando and the Bahamas and from Miami PD, he knows about those two bank transfers, us being behind the bankers' murders outside Coral Gables and that we murdered Officers Orion, Gierek and Cantrell. When Calvera and Batista find out we have two hundred million dollars of their money, they'll put a contract out on us. I suggest we withdraw that money from our accounts and return it to the arms dealers and tell them we had no knowledge this was mob money."

"Return it to the arms dealers?" Smith exclaimed. "You must be kidding!"

"I'm not kidding," Ross said. "We return the money and take the next flight from Florida to Mexico. We have no choice."

"We must head for twenty-three Palm Lane as soon as we've been to the bank," Smith agreed.

***

At 23 Palm Lane, Amy, Helen and Patricia were in the hideout's basement, their arms tied behind their backs with strong straps and their mouths taped. They were lying slumped on a double bed. Amy and Patricia struggled with the straps, but their fully exposed foreheads and feminine faces tightened up with pain as the straps dug into their wrists. Communicating by humming noises through the strips of white tape covering their mouths, they pulled themselves toward each other, their backs and arms joined. Amy's hands touched Helen's wrists and started to unfasten the strap tying her wrists, pulling the buttons out of the holes. With all the buttons out, Amy slipped the strap through the buckle and loosened Helen's hands. Helen was free. She threw the strap onto the bed, then untied Patricia's hands.

The temperature in the basement was freezing cold, and Patricia and Amy felt the chill on their bare faces, so Patricia unfastened her ponytail to let her black hair hang over her face and neck. With Amy humming through the tape with irritation, Patricia untied Amy's ponytail so her brunette hair hung down to her shoulders, covering her face and neck, but the women's foreheads were still exposed to the chilly conditions. The three women were only wearing jeans and sweatshirts, with no vests or T-shirts underneath.

Patricia loosened the strap around Amy's hands, unfastened it and dumped it on the bed. The women were about to tear the tape from their mouths when they heard the basement door open and five rough-looking men came down the steps, four of them bearded and one mustached. Leaving the tape covering their mouths to silence their terrified breathing, Amy, Helen and Patricia quietly seized three bricks from the basement's corner and hid behind an old, disused closet. The men, all Cubans, entered the room and approached the bed, but found only the black straps. Running up behind the men, Amy, Helen and Patricia swung the bricks into three of their heads with all their strength. The impact of the blows was so violent, the Cubans' heads split open, blood gushing down their faces, and the bearded brutes fell to the floor. The other two Cubans spun round, reaching for their handguns, but Amy stabbed her fingernails into one man's eyes and then punched him in the throat, snapping his windpipe. Patricia's fist crunched three times into the other guy's nose until the soft bone cracked into his skull, blood spurting from the brute's nostrils. With a hand strike, she slammed the bridge of his nose through his head and into his brain.

Both Cubans died within ten seconds, one from a fractured windpipe, the other from brain damage. They collapsed to the floor and lay beside the three Cubans whose heads had been bashed open by the bricks. Amy, Helen and Patricia pulled the tape away from their mouths and then seized the Cubans' handguns.

"Damn it, Patricia," Amy whispered. "Why did you waste time undoing your hair and mine when we have to get out of here?"

"My face and forehead are cold, and so are yours," Patricia snapped. "Our hair would warm up our faces and necks. The temperature in here is freezing, and we're only wearing sweatshirts and jeans."

"This is no time to argue," Helen said. "We must escape whilst the coast is clear."

"Before we do that, just one question," Amy said.

"Go on."

"Is my lipstick smudged from where my mouth was taped?"

"Yes, and so's mine!" Patricia snapped. "But this is not the time or place for something so petty!"

"No, we must go," Helen whispered. "Are you ready? We'll head up the steps, fight any Cubans in the hallway and then escape through the front door."

The women silently ran up the steps and found themselves in the hallway, but before they could leave, the doorbell rang. They retreated into the kitchen and hid behind the wall, flanking the kitchen's open door, clutching the Cubans' handguns. Calvera, Batista and four bearded Cubans pulled open the front door. Lieutenants Ross and Smith were at the door.

"Ross and Smith!" Calvera snarled.

"We have your two hundred million bucks," Ross growled.

"Money Chief Mills stole from your Bahamas offshore account before we murdered him," Smith said.

The female cops hiding in the kitchen gasped with shock at this revelation.

"You expect us to be happy?" Batista hissed.

"After you stole our money on Mills's behalf, popped Mills, took the money for yourselves and then blamed everything on Mills?" Calvera growled. "And you expect us to let you walk away without us pumping lead into you! Not a chance!"

Calvera and Batista pressed their handguns into the cops' stomachs.

"No, don't do this!" Ross exclaimed. "We can come to a deal!"

"No way!" Calvera replied.

Calvera and Batista squeezed the triggers and each pumped two deafening gunshots into the cops' guts, then three shots into their chests. With blood spattering onto the arms dealers' leather jackets and staining their jeans, both brutes grinned as Ross and Smith fell against the wall and slumped awkwardly to the floor, trails of blood smearing the wall from the exit wounds in their backs.

Then the squad van and two civilian cars raced to a halt in the driveway. Dave and Tony scrambled out of one civilian car whilst CSI Officers Houston, Jackson, Watts and Cornelli emerged from the second vehicle. Squad Leader Erikson and Officers Brogan, Harmon and Dill hurried out of the squad van, and all ten cops sprinted toward the front door. The bearded Cubans were about to slam the door shut to keep the police officers out, but Amy, Helen and Patricia raced out of the kitchen, aimed the handguns and blasted toward the Cubans. Amy fired five exploding shots into two Cubans whilst Helen fired another three into the third thug and Patricia blazed three gunshots into the fourth brute. All these Cubans were blasted through the doorway and fell flat onto the steps.

Calvera and Batista fled into the side room, then the back room and through to the hideout's garden. In the garden was a helicopter in which these criminals would escape from Florida.

Twenty-one other mobsters were positioned on the green, and as Calvera and Batista climbed into the helicopter and started the engine, they ordered their gang to cover their escape by confronting the police officers charging through the kitchen and back room. The propellers started spinning, and the helicopter rose from the grass.

The mob pulled open the doors of both rooms overlooking the garden, with eleven crooks aiming their AK-47 assault rifles into the kitchen and ten criminals storming into the back room, rifles raised.

The seven men and women from Vice were ready for the first assault and repeatedly fired their revolvers and handguns. Taking the initiative, Erikson took down three thugs with headshots. They fell against three other crooks in spasms of death. Brogan blasted five revolver shots into these criminals, two bullets striking the heads of two riflemen and three puncturing the chest of a third.

The last five gunmen ejected a ferocious hail of bullets toward the seven vice cops, who instantly dived to the floor. Harmon and Dill aimed their revolvers upwards. Two blasts from Harmon's piece penetrated a gunman's chest before another three sent bullets into a mobster's solar plexus. Both brutes hurtled backward onto the kitchen patio. Dill fired four shots from his revolver, one rupturing a mobster's head and three rounds puncturing another guy's chest and abdomen. Both brutes slammed with force against the last criminal and fell against the wall.

The surviving mobster blazed nine savage rifle shots toward Erikson, Brogan, Harmon and Dill, who rolled underneath the table while the women fired their handguns. A hail of shots bloodied the gunman's chest and shoulders, and the brute fell to the patio outside the kitchen door. The kitchen floor, wall and patio were smeared and soaked with pools of blood.

The ten mobsters who'd blazed with ferocious blasts of their rifles into the back room were firing over the heads of Dave, Tony and the CSI detectives, who were kneeling on the floor. They retaliated fast. Houston blasted a criminal's chest and head with four gunshots, whilst Jackson vomited five blasts, Watts five and Cornelli six, the three black cops bloodying the chests and stomachs of three mobsters. The impact slammed the brutes violently against the six killers firing from behind.

Dave and Tony were firing at the same time. Tony pumped two rifle shots into the heads of two criminals and three into a third guy's chest. With blood billowing from their terrible wounds, all three brutes crashed against the wall or through the back door and were dead in five seconds. Firing his own rifle with ruthless brutality, Dave alternated his gunfire between mobsters, the bullets puncturing their stomachs and shoulders so the mobsters were crippled with agony. With four more bullets to a mobster's chest, six through another brute's solar plexus and the last five dealing the same horrific injuries to his third opponent, Dave dropped the last three mobsters. Their bodies slammed violently against the wall.

Dave and Tony raced to their feet and hurried through the back door to see the arms dealers escaping in the helicopter. Dave fired five shots after them and Tony another three, whilst Erikson, Brogan and Harmon released a total of fifteen gunshots, but the helicopter was too far away.

"They escaped," Tony growled.

"Calvera and Batista slipped through our fingers," Dave said. His tone was bitter. "Are the women cops okay?"

"Yes, they are," Brogan said.

"They took on many mobsters before we arrived," Harmon replied.

"Their shooting was cool, really cool." Dill chuckled.

"Your shooting was cool, Dill," Erikson added. "Your former vice squad taught you well. Your expertise with a handgun was as brutal as that of Officers Brogan and Harmon, who also fought well."

Amy, Helen and Patricia wrapped their arms around Officers Brogan, Harmon and Dill and violently kissed their faces, tears flowing down the women's faces. Then they laughed with joy, hugging the men with all their strength.

"Thanks for rescuing us." Amy chuckled. "I knew you'd come for us eventually."

"And we also thank Dave, Tony and Houston's CSI officers." Helen laughed.

"Especially Dave and Tony," Patricia told the Feds. "The best FBI agents in Florida."

The women approached Dave and Tony and their lips met the men's faces with nervous kisses.

"You women should take credit too," Dave pointed out. "How you took on a gang of Cubans in the basement and four Cubans who were about to slam the front door on us. Your shooting was as professional as that of Erikson, Brogan, Harmon and Dill."

"It was us FBI agents who discovered the location of Calvera's hideout," Tony said. "Through tracing Calvera's calls here at the call center. The good news is Calvera and Batista murdered Ross and Smith before we could arrest and prosecute these police officers, but the bad news is both mobsters escaped in a helicopter and are still at large."

"We'll nail them some other time," Dave remarked.

"We know you will," Houston agreed.

"Good luck to you, Dave, Tony," Dill said. "At least now, the murders of Officers Orion, Gierek and Cantrell have been avenged, and Amy especially can have closure for her husband's death."

Amy smiled modestly, and Helen and Patricia grinned.

"The mobsters have met their Vietnam," Tony said.

"But more arms dealers, drug dealers and pimps will replace them," Dave added. "You CSI detectives must carry out forensics work at this hideout whilst the rest of us check on Captain Robert Siffrey at the hospital."

"We're on it," Houston replied.

***

At Miami's Mount Sinai Hospital, the FBI agents and vice cops paid Captain Siffrey a visit. The bearded black cop had recovered enormously. He was now conscious and eating jelly and ice cream.

"Hi guys," Siffrey greeted Dave and Tony. "I'm ready to run the department, as long as Mills, Ross and Smith don't get in my way."

"They're not around anymore," Dave replied.

"Feel free to run the department," Tony invited Siffrey. "You've earned the right, as much as Nicole Lamenski earned the right to run Timlook PD."

Erikson, Brogan, Harmon and Dill grinned with joy, and smiles also broke across the faces of Amy, Helen and Patricia.

"All these officers, led by Dave and Tony, rescued us from our kidnappers, Calvera and Batista and their mobsters." Amy chuckled. "We all took down those evil men. But Calvera and Batista got away."

"They got away!" Siffrey exclaimed.

"Yes, they did," Dave replied. "But whatever it takes, Tony and I will get them."

Siffrey shook Dave's hand with a tight grip, a gesture of respect.

What Did You Think of *Bent on Justice?*

A big thank you for purchasing this book. It means a lot that you chose this book specifically from such a wide range on offer. I do hope you enjoyed it.

Book reviews are incredibly important for an author. All feedback helps them improve their writing for future projects and for developing this edition. If you are able to spare a few minutes to post a review on Amazon, that would be much appreciated.

Publisher Information

Rowanvale Books provides publishing services to independent authors, writers and poets all over the globe. We deliver a personal, honest and efficient service that allows authors to see their work published, while remaining in control of the process and retaining their creativity. By making publishing services available to authors in a cost-effective and ethical way, we at Rowanvale Books hope to ensure that the local, national and international community benefits from a steady stream of good quality literature.

For more information about us, our authors or our publications, please get in touch.

www.rowanvalebooks.com
info@rowanvalebooks.com

www.ingramcontent.com/pod-product-compliance
Lightning Source LLC
Chambersburg PA
CBHW051112050726
47592CB00002B/780